MYSTERY IN S

John Hartley Williams is the author of seven collections of poetry, most recently *Spending Time with Walter* (2001). He teaches English at the Free University of Berlin, where he has been since 1976.

John Hartley Williams

MYSTERY IN SPIDERVILLE

A Romance

VINTAGE

Published by Vintage 2003

2 4 6 8 10 9 7 5 3 1

First published in Great Britain in 2002 by
Jonathan Cape

Vintage
Random House, 20 Vauxhall Bridge Road,
London SW1V 2SA

Random House Australia (Pty) Limited
20 Alfred Street, Milsons Point, Sydney
New South Wales 2061, Australia

Random House New Zealand Limited
18 Poland Road, Glenfield,
Auckland 10, New Zealand

Random House (Pty) Limited
Endulini, 5A Jubilee Road, Parktown 2193,
South Africa

The Random House Group Limited Reg. No. 954009
www.randomhouse.co.uk

A CIP catalogue record for this book
is available from the British Library

ISBN 0 099 42693 5

Papers used by Random House are natural, recyclable
products made from wood grown in sustainable forests.
The manufacturing processes conform to the environ-
mental regulations of the country of origin

Printed and bound in Great Britain by
Cox & Wyman Limited, Reading, Berkshire

He's a monster born in the brothel, who stands eternally on a pedestal. Although he's alive, he's nevertheless part of the museum. He's not ugly. His face is even attractive, very dark, oriental in complexion. There's a good deal of pink and green in him. He squats, but in a bizarre, twisted pose. Wound several times around him, like a big snake, is something of a blackish hue. I ask him what it is. He tells me it's a huge appendix that comes out of his head, rubbery and elastic and so long, so very long, that if he coiled it on top of his head like a pigtail it would be much too heavy and absolutely impossible to carry – so he has to wind it round his limbs, which actually gives a better effect. I converse for quite a while with this monster. He shares his anxieties and sorrows with me. For several years now, he's been obliged to present himself in this room, on this pedestal, to the public's curious gaze. But his main problem is at dinner time. As a living creature, he's obliged to eat with the whores of the place, tottering along with his rubber appendage to the dining-room, where he has to keep it round him, or place it like a spool of rope on a chair, taking care not to let it drag on the ground in case it pulls him over backwards. In addition to this he's short and squat, yet he has to eat beside a tall, well-built tart. He tells me the whole story, what's more, without bitterness. I don't dare to touch him, but I find him interesting.

Charles Baudelaire
Lettre à Charles Asselineau
[Paris] Jeudi 13 mars 1856
Tr. JHW

What a man has to do, he has to

meet his mother in hell

Charles Olson, 'O'Ryan 6'

CONTENTS

MYSTERY IN SPIDERVILLE

THE BED

You make it, you lie on it. I do, anyway. I'm in the seventh-floor dwelling of a run-down apartment building. There are pigeons on the flaking sill outside. The bedroom has four walls, four papery sourcloth, cheesepink walls. Stars everywhere, to remind me of why I'm here. Also a used condom under the bed. Above me, the ceiling spreads its carpet of dull gold. There's also, naturally, a door.

I lie on the bed. I'm waiting for what I do not want to happen to happen. For the door to open. Through a thin wall, I can hear voices, brilliant with communication, with laughter and murder. I'm certain it's Spider, exchanging his essence with whoever might be foolish enough to believe him.

Truth is a holy flame.

I'm aware of it burning next door. I've no intention of getting too close.

Spider is enjoying himself. He's exploring the nature of those around him, slipping the hooks and eyes of people's minds, curious to see what might fall out. The solution to the puzzle of my existence, he thinks, is to be found in an object discarded by someone who has undressed much too hurriedly, an earring, a clip or a brooch.

Can you imagine him bending down to examine a minute yet precisely coiled artefact observed upon the carpet?

I am a hairpin.

Naked as I am, I'm certainly no sight for the men in hats and the women in raincoats who stumble in from the street, down the corridor outside, to recapitulate finally what love has done to them under the silent and white umbrella of darkness.

I try to imagine her as she was, touching my eyes with her tongue. Her hair was slightly foetid, like leaves. She pinned it back, casually, at the brow. No, I am not now, nor at any other time, being caressed. Nor do I hope for or have any presentiment that would lead to small touches of her mouth to mine. My emptiness is full as the room.

Spider! Spider! Hold on to the truth!

ROOM SERVICE

The pain of this location (Alarum Heights) jabs my shoulder like a nerve.

Is it something to be breathed over by cigarette-stained men in the quiet puzzled investigation room of judgement day?

I try to pull the bedclothes over me. I was always trying to do that, but they merely slide away from me, as if the most important thing in the world were the acute recovery of my nakedness.

Spider, I know, is not sleeping.

He has that old jacket for comfort, that impregnated jacket, made of the thread of old woman's hair, of the cloth from a soldier's combat clothes, of a thick weave, its collar patchworked with fur, a jacket steeped in tiredness – the tiredness that comes from years, yes, years of the old task: self-preservation.

Spider's fists are entombed in its pockets.

I should wear to bed what I wear in the world, but I don't. As the light fades, I disguise myself. I change my teeth, my skin, my dreams, my soul, anything. My pyjamas pulse with chameleon colours. I change myself over and over in bright complicity with the darkness until the darkness wins and I sink into the nothingness of sleep.

Spider never sleeps, yet when he considers the contents of his wardrobe he does so with heavy eyes. His wardrobe is a museum of sleep, and Spider is its curator. He reaches in and selects one dreamless garment after another. He wears only what's old, what gets older as he wears it, never throwing things away, the older the useder, the useder the better, with a slight smile on his face.

He's wider awake than time itself.

Meanwhile, the throbbing structure of this building remains unaltered, in cold altercation with the sky, my unmoving position, here, on this bed . . .

STROLLING SPIDER

Spider has a walk which is half prowl, half shuffle. His spine curves forward into the wind as if the weight of his head were too heavy for the stalk, his lips move as if a breeze were stirring them, his hands are thrust straight-elbowed into the deep chambers of his pockets where his digits lie softly curled and only one mild finger plays gently with the pleasurable softness of himself. He *BOUNCES* as he walks, up on his toes and down again, half blind he must be as he walks, one sleepy eye in the top of his head, never missing the feel, the flow, the flare of the blank world around him.

His muttering attracts remarks, but it's true, honest muttering, not the rambling of the mad. It's a prelude to the shout to come, full of tiny attentiveness to the dwarfish imprecations of his own mind, down an alley, against a brick wall, or anywhere out there where the wind might take a sign advertising overeating at low prices and drive it along the kerb causing Spider to skip out of the way, no shadow of a laugh crossing the slope of his face.

Watch him. He still continues muttering. In the World Cafe Bar Grill Pizzeria and Strip, which offers its shabby occupants a single uninterrupted chance to mutter their way through the stale reality of waiting, he stares at the listless food. The long queue shuffles between bright chromium rails. With his wooden tray in one hand, he gropes for a plate of illustrated sausages under a glass case, staring at the discrepancy between the picture and the chipolatas in the vague, hurt-pleasured way of one who longs for the warmth of Spain. What a cosmic parody of the inexplicably dissatisfied customer! When I see that caricature of a hooded twinkle in his sunken eye-sockets, I shudder. I note his performance. I see a man enacting his own self-burial. He's up to his scrawny neck in loathsome relish.

Yet somewhere, beyond the pictures of paradisal locations on the walls, beyond the exotic decor, the gaily diverting price lists, the wittily scrumptious packaging of dull necessities, his muttering, of which all in the queue are becoming insistently aware, begins to render the bright city of Eldorado visible, so that between what is and what is not muttered you can almost see the truth.

Something like that, anyway.

Eating a mustard-smeared banger encased in the coffin of a bun, his mouth open, yellow stains on his upper lip and collar, Spider leaves the cafeteria. He slouches down the street, his coat wafting behind him. A red-leather-upholstered hoodless limousine swishes past. It is driven by powerful loudspeakers which stun the eardrums of passers-by and make them collectively wish it gone. Next to the driver, who is wearing a yellow shirt, a flowing red noose around his

neck, a Mephistopheles beard and billy-goat spec-
tacles, are two women in white chiffon blouses
through which the heavy roll of their breasts is visible,
the push of their nipples against the material like a
boy's nose pressed up against a window. Catching
Spider's goggling contemplation, they throw open
their wraparound skirts and part their legs. His mouth
is arrested in mid-chew. They wear no underclothes,
and he gazes deeply into two richly black-plumed
fleeces, held prettily open by scarlet-lacquered fingernails, an invitation to a rave or a beheading, the
women screeching with laughter as the limousine
rounds the corner, the driver bellowing and roaring,
and Spider enquiring of a passer-by between resumed
yet stupefied munches of his bun:

'Did you see that?'

LOCAL COLOUR

I have slept badly, hearing the wind rattle the window frame. She draws her fingers gently down my body, touches me alive again.

We take a bath together, our legs interfolded. Warm rays of sunlight pour through the window, also filling the tub. On the sixth floor, below us, we can hear Mrs Limbo abusing Mr Limbo. On the ground floor live Mr and Mrs Swack. They don't like me. They don't like my beloved. When she runs up the stairs in those tight pants, that loose blouse open at the throat, they stare at her. They'd like to destroy us. They'd like to burn us at the stake.

I'm dressed now, on my way to the market round the corner. As clouds gather, I buy salad tomatoes. A Japanese man and his wife take a photograph of me. A typical scene in old Europe. Some drops fall on their lenses and on my face. Was that a touch of April snow? Making my way home, I imagine a more contemplative artist setting up his easel, appraising the subject. Mr and Mrs Swack glare at me as I re-enter the building. My beloved is still in her silk dressing-gown. In a wayward fall, her brown hair shapes and shades her cheeks. I pull on the cord, open the pale, creamy-coloured folds of it, and cup her breasts in my hands. Our tongues drag the pools of our mouths for the little corpses we have drowned there. Locked together, we totter to the bed and fall upon it. How boring, how divine – that struggle to get out of one's clothes! We're like languorous detectives, investigating speed. She's naked again and her body fills my hands as if intended for no other purpose. I let my mouth rove across her stomach, draw my tongue down the slit of her, and she turns over, raising her selfless flanks to me so that I have two entrances before me and stall, not knowing which to choose. I yearn, forensically, for what is irresponsible and beautiful and hidden. In the silent rooms of Alarum Heights, the other occupants listen to her cries. Let April do what it wants. Snowflakes one minute, disconsolate sunbeams the next. We're alone in the landscape of ourselves and the artist is utterly preoccupied, making us the whole canvas, obliterating the crags and the weather. Ah, the soft, lascivious strokes of the brush! Such shuddering collusion, such painful eagerness . . . She gasps. She's all light and air and her skin is warm and sweet, like new bread, and her body deep.

OFFICE SPIDER

Spider is a clerk of metamorphoses. Most of the day he sits in the office with his hat on reading *Cars Illustrated*. At night, however, he goes home to a grave. He sleeps soundly. A nice, comfortable rectangle in a churchyard. Well before daybreak, moles flee as the turf counterpane beneath which he lies shudders and crumples. He wakes and sits up, earth skittering off his bones. With a dry rattle, he stands and performs his morning exercises, fingerbone to toebone, spine-clicking stretches. Once his skeleton is limber and dancing in its sockets, he looks round for the rest of him. He keeps his internal organs moist and juicy by folding them into a dampened potato sack, and now he takes them out, one by one. He holds his heart up to his ear and shakes it until the tick resumes. With his bony feet well apart to avoid the drips, he squeezes out his kidneys. Two hoarse puffs into his lungs and they start to wheeze their cracked hornpipe. He assembles the jigsaw puzzle of his glands and places it behind his ribcage. Coiling his intestine like string round one elbow and the V of his thumb and forefinger, he lowers it into the cradle of his abdomen. Then from the branches of a yew tree, he takes down the empty pouch of his skin

– he always sleeps naked – and pulls it over his head. A wriggle and it fits, tight and smooth. He adjusts the angle of his nose, pops in his eyes and does a roll on his lips with two fingers. He's a white throb on the dark earth, echoing the first pulse of dawn. Bats pipistrello through the tower of the adjacent church belfry. He gives a pale, cold and moony smile followed by a distinctive yawp. The yawp of a man whose toilette is finally completed.

Of course, he can't turn up at the office like this. An unclothed man behind a desk is an affront to the world of affairs. With a powerful suck of breath, he vacuums the leaves off a nearby tree and fashions a suit out of them. The latest range. From a piece of rotted tree bark, he makes a briefcase. Two stale cowpats become elegant moccasins. He slides his feet into them. He's a craftsman of mud. A wicker couturier.

As the sun heaves itself over Gibbet Hill, Spider crunches down gravel paths, through the lych-gate, to where his motor car (an extremely thin one, year of manufacture 1946) is parked. Then he's off to work, in a halting series of jerks and smoke-spluttering bangs. At work is where we'll leave him, more or less where we came in, sitting in his office, leafing though a copy of *Cars Illustrated*. Or dreamlessly staring into space, perhaps, high above his designated bay in the office car park, which has exactly the same dimensions as the unmarked grave he sleeps in . . .

SPRINGTIME IN THE CITY

Needing a new beak parer, I walk down to the Falconry Shop, the peregrine on my wrist. After a heavy storm, lilac petals are everywhere. In high apartment buildings, turned-back beds are cooling, their sheets stripped and folded, their pillows plumped out. It's foetid inside the shop, with the smell of birds. I buy new talon scissors as well as the beak parer, exchange information about how best to control the pigeon population, and emerge blinking into damp air through which a heavy perfume rises. Still clutching their umbrellas, stepping delicately aside to avoid their puddled reflections, people seem aimless, wandering ineffectually into shop doorways, trying to recover their sense of place and time.

I cross the street, my raincoat flapping. It's suddenly brilliant and warm, and the peregrine stares straight up, blinklessly, into the sun. When the bus comes, it's crowded with people, inhaling the damp odour of each other's clothes. Their faces wear migraine smiles of doubt. You sense pressure, suffocation, hay fever everywhere. The bird looks straight ahead. People stare at its talons, hooked in my leather bracelet.

I alight near the park and she comes towards me, takes my arm, and we walk together. People nod to us and greet us, though they can't have seen us before. I nod back. It's the presence of the bird which makes us familiar to them. I can see skateboarders wheeling and ducking around a scooped-out arena of concrete and we stop to watch. The bird shifts uneasily, following the skateboarders as they crouch, jump and twist. I realise she's no longer beside me. From the far side of the arena, she's waving back at me gaily. The whole city is like a headscarf she wears round her throat.

I release the bird and watch it fly off. It dwindles towards the clouds.

Deciding it's time to make a declaration, an exhibition of myself, I borrow a skateboard off an indolent teenager, spread my arms and, imitating the hawk, launch myself downward into the basin, bracing my knees as I gather speed. My plan is to ascend the opposite incline on a swashbuckling curve and at the apogee of my momentum, just where she's standing, come to a dead stop, bow, and then perform an arabesque of deference and homage before her.

I'm in a great bowl, lilac and rainy.

As I ascend towards her watching smile, my arms spread, my raincoat trailing like a vampire's cloak, I catch sight of Spider in a black hat and galoshes, standing next to her. With his hands raised beside his left ear, he's clapping ironically, patting his left palm with his right fingertips. He resembles wisdom's half-witted brother. His yellow teeth are like the verdict at somebody's trial. Behind him, where the ramparts of the city are jagged against the sky, I glimpse a small notice to his right, which reads: *You are now entering Spiderville*. I come to a dead stop, acknowledge them both, do a neat swivel, pause, and go swooping down.

Descending, I feel the peregrine alight on my shoulder, feathering to keep its balance, the soft brush of its wingtip against my ear . . .

SPIDER'S NATURE

He's everywhere. Lift a dead leaf in the forest, turn over a stone in the field, open the door of that store room in the cellar – you're sure to find him. Sometimes he spreads his webs flat on the ground, sometimes he prefers heights. Occasionally, he lives at mountain altitudes, or unpigmented and blind in caves. Often, you'll find him crouched in the angle of a wall, behind wardrobes, on window panes.

The purpose of the web he spins is both home and a trap. The silk is an endless reel of thread, like the ribbon Ariadne gave Theseus. At the centre of this tripwire domicile, Spider sits motionless, awaiting the slight vibration which might indicate a capture. He consumes actresses, oracles, priestesses and women who are half-wolf dancers of the failed round of life.

Young girls are a speciality of his. Boys arouse the beginning of an irony. The fleas in cheap hotels disgust him. Businessmen are a delectation.

Traversing the interiors of large, gloomy houses at evening, spreading a quite unjustified terror, Spider is no more and no less than a male looking for company. When the band strikes up and he begins to dance, the prolonged and complex manoeuvres of his step are designed to confirm that he corresponds biologically to his chosen mate so she will not consider him vulgar prey and eat him.

Often Spider brings the gift of a silk-wrapped sweet and mates with his partner while she is eating it. If no sweet is available, a pebble will do. He departs swiftly afterwards lest a gang of vengeful females arrives. His behaviour during webweaving, hunting and courtship is so elaborate that to all intents and purposes it defeats itself. One should not, therefore, conclude it is a mark of intelligence. Maybe Spider's behaviour is a series of instinctive acts, following one another in a genetically predetermined succession.

What predetermined it is difficult to say.

Spiderlings, should they occur, quickly abandon the gregariousness of the nest and start early on to exhibit blind individualism. These juveniles disperse by a process called ballooning. Releasing strands of silk which are picked up by the wind, they are carried away on their own threads.

They are unable, obviously, to control the direction in which the wind carries them.

HER BREASTS

Dawn is breaking over rubbish, over ironmongery, scrap merchandise, towers of bald auto tyres, the lapsed dreams of dealers in old refrigerators and leaky washing machines. I pass the silent cars where, in this junk hideaway, the young oblige the old at midnight. I hear the falsified promises over and over again, smell the stale cigarette butts, see the three-quarters-empty bottles, used needles, shameless photographs, all the scurrilous affidavits of an inexplicable future.

A parliament of birds is debating viciously as an icy sun comes up over the tin fence. Chirrup chirrup. I am the janitor and as I walk my pockets jingle with rusted keys, wire picklocks, tiny tools, all the instrumentation of official and unofficial entry. I fling open the gates to this memory-deserted yard and peer down the empty street outside.

Nothing.

Walking back, I think how oily my hair is, smell the runaway-stallion stink of my crotch. What words can I use to describe those scuffles out there on the scrubland, those greasy depletions of myself? I walk along, jangling, my mind a blank. Only the birds sound pleased with themselves. As well they might.

I press my face to the rear window of a crashed car.

She is sitting sideways along the back seat, wearing a blue woollen donkey jacket and nothing else. Her bare legs are drawn up, pressed together, and her eyes meet mine. The sun is cold upon my back.

Slowly, with arrogant deliberateness, she opens her jacket and takes the gaze of my eyes into the plural custody of her breasts.

Inside, I can see the leather seats are stained with last night's brief, sour excitement.

I walk back to my hut, with a shuffling tread. Spider is tending the coke furnace, stooped over the fire, warming his face to a reddened glow. He has taken vows of poverty and silence. My monkish, intractable companion. He cannot and must not know my thoughts.

In my thoughts, of course, her slender fingers move upwards across her hips, her palms slide under the frail swing of her breasts, she offers me her yearning aureoles. My mind fastens itself to her. I close my eyes. Time was never as perfect as this.

SPIDER SPOTS A FLAW

On the door it says Detective Inspector J. Spider Rembrandt. Push open the door, quietly, you don't want to wake him. In the old wooden swivel chair behind his completely empty desk, he's leaning back, his eyes closed. The nostrils through which he's inhaling the dusty air are pointed at the ceiling, and his lips burble slightly as he expels the effortful conclusions of his reverie. In his half-dream, he's tiptoeing towards the logic-undoing surprise that lurks in every revelation of the unconscious. With trembling fingers, he's lifting a minuscule clue with tweezers, depositing it under a microscope to establish whose sperm, hair, blood group it belongs to. He may appear dead to the world, but actually he's totally alert to the moment when, midway between wakefulness and sleep, he traps the fly of an idea, alights on the hairy loveliness of a clue, whips off the sheet and reveals the victim for who she is – down to the last goosebump.

His eyes blink open. This is what he's been waiting for. Grabbing a sketch-book, he begins to draw the exquisite corpse. She bears a lively yet defunct resemblance to a vanished person whose death has merely been mooted, whom he has never seen, and whose body has never been recovered. A youngish woman, tall, with brown hair. Next comes the crime scene. He delineates a dock at midnight. Steel cranes on rusting tracks stand high above the harbour. The reflection of a steamer ripples in the moon-choppy water. A sinister glow covers all. She's reclining on an empty pallet as if in the languor of post-coital desire, an arm flung out upon the puddled sheet of a tarpaulin. There's no mark of violence upon her. Swiftly widening the net of his Venus pencil, Spider captures the cold circumstances of her demise. Somewhere between hulking warehouses, a rat-like figure scuttles. In pencil pursuit, with deep-scored slashes and arcs, Spider makes the murderer's white face surface from a sea of shadows. It wears the agonised look of one who has just realised he has sacrificed a million opportunities to a single moment of individualistic error. Spider chuckles. He loves to nab a desperado. With amused ferocity, he scrawls a lightning circle round that homicidal countenance. A torchbeam of truth, it pins the perpetrator to a grimy wall.

Suddenly, his scribbling hand desists. His eyebrows meet in the middle. He strikes his brow with his fist, nearly blinding himself with the pencil in the process.

Damn! The murder weapon! Where is it?

THE WISDOM OF POETS

The peregrine's beak taps at the window. I peer out
and note the scattered feathers on the lawn. I return
to the bed and the piles of books surrounding it.

We should get drunk, the poet says. On wine,
poetry or virtue, whichever you prefer.

I brood on the woman who left me. She did not
understand the significance of that terribly deep and
adoring act of faithlessness of mine. It was only a
drunken moment in a taxi. When the cab roared off
with a flourish of spray, drenching me, the oval of a
face whitening the smoked rear window, I felt as if
I had recently shot myself. I stared up at the lit lamp
on the seventh floor. She was waiting for me.

I took the lift. Walked down the corridor. Searched
my pocket for the keys. There was only this bed, that
window. How often we had surrendered our flesh
to one another in this very room! Like pigeons to
hawks . . .

Turning the poet's page in silence, I notice the
absent counterpoint of coos.

She was tall, slim-waisted, with heavy breasts, delicate nipples. Sometimes Spider, who is an excellent
mimic, imitates that deep, slightly petulant voice, and
calls me up pretending to be her. He reminds me

her submissiveness was really just a camouflage for bloodlust. We were made for each other. I recall how, in that moment when she and I wrenched ourselves apart, the world was full of an empty yearning, breaking its fingernails on the brickwork of the city, how I stared at the sexual publicity all over town and bit down hard on its winsome representations of desire. Spider gives a yelp of surprise.

Wine, poetry and virtue — what does he know about such things?

It takes a drunken woman to satisfy my mind. Her willingness to surrender everything is the unemptiable bottle I ply her with. When she's naked and has abandoned herself to all the suggestions I care to make, her every movement becomes a line of poetry scrawled on the whiteness of the sheets. Those dashed-off forms are made as easily as one would make an unpremeditated visit to the hairdresser's. I stare at the extraordinary wild forest her light brown hair has become.

A woman who likes to get drunk, who surrenders the poetry of her soul to my rude, versatile flesh.

And Spider thinks I'm just some fellow he can annoy at will.

UP IN THE AIR

It's a bore to have to climb the outside of a building to reach one's seventh floor apartment, but there it is. I've lost my keys again and the front door of Alarum Heights is always kept locked on Sundays – the porter takes his wife to lunch at Doggo's – so there I am, a human fly.

'You're so predictable,' says Spider. 'Everywhere, the aftermath of your perfectly foreseeable lapses of attention. Yes, yes, your keys. I know. Look at the ghostly matrices your inattentive selves have left behind: phantom holes in what should have been a history. You're a non-history. A serial sieve. Forgetting, omitting, hesitating till it's too late: just contemplate those failed enactments of what should have been necessity – a crowd of ghosts, wailing and chattering and wringing their hands, waiting to be performed in your next life, if you get one.'

Below me in the car park, a small crowd has gathered to watch my ascent. A gaggle of past selves, perhaps, staring up at the future they were all so desperate to avoid. I don't much care for having phantoms summoned at a time like this. Besides, the next handhold looks distinctly precarious.

Spider continues in that loathsomely reasonable

tone of his: 'Well, you do put effort into what you do, I'll say that, even though the actual doing usually turns out to be the reverse of accomplishment, the disenactment of what needs to be done. Striving to reach a summit, however, is laudable in itself. I think every citizen should have a dream. But don't wake up. Wakefulness is rarely amusing.'

He's right in this respect. I'm wide awake, gritting my teeth, and keyless. My right arm is flung above my head, my left hand grips a sill downwards to my left. My right knee's at an acute angle; my left leg's straight as an arrow. I resemble a paralysed bolt of lightning. The city's much too far below. Only one word accurately describes my position: stuck.

Spider has glistening threads connected to his forearms, thighs and abdomen. Suspended on the tiny wires he extrudes from himself, he's gravely clownish, climbing the shining rope of himself, then letting himself fall in comical abandon. Going up, going down – it's all the same to him. Of course, being an arachnid he remembers everything. His world is too tiny to be forgotten. He remembers every heave of himself, every lowering, every grass blade, twig or windowsill. He can't stop remembering me, for example. If only I could get him to forget.

There's an orgy going on in the fourth floor, one of those parties where people take unlabelled tablets and throw themselves out of the window in the conviction they can fly. That's no part of my agenda. All I want to do is climb back to my apartment, enter through a window, breathe the aura of the vanished presence in which it is steeped, revisit the scene of my furious, contemplative indolence – a scene I will always come back to, even after I'm dead.

'My, my,' says Spider. 'You *are* an aspiring ghost, aren't you?'

If I had a pair of scissors I'd snip those threads of his. But I haven't.

In my stuck position I breathe deeply. An aroma, something herbal mixed with rain, something of crushed damp grass, something of an undergarment retaining the fragrance of intimate surrenders, something of sodden rope, something of the odour of anguish . . . some deeply impregnated and personal article that I can't quite identify . . . some aroma, anyway, wafts into my nostrils.

How long have I been up here? I've lost count of the floor I've reached. Is this the sixth?

'It is. And the next bit's tricky,' Spider murmurs. 'Another heave and you confront the truth. Are you ready?'

I am. And I'm not. My predicament returns to me with the force of a ricocheted bullet. All my windows are, of course, locked on the inside; how then do I hope to enter through them? As for my keys – I recall this with self-lacerating exactitude – they are exactly where I left them. In the glove compartment of my Ariadne Chronospeed Excursion Mk II *Coupe de Ville*.

How redundant can you get?

BAND OF GOLD

Stop me, if you've heard this one.

We get a late arrival in the hotel one evening. A woman with a mane of reddish-brown hair comes in and says: 'There's a small chest on the back seat of the taxi. Please carry it upstairs for me.'

I carry the chest for her, follow her gorgeous, long legs up the stairs, fall to my knees on the threadbare carpet, and beg her to be mine.

'You'll have to pass a test first.'

'Anything!'

'I want you to travel on with my chest, following a strict itinerary. I've hired a chauffeur, who will call for it tomorrow morning. When you come to the next hotel, you must place it in a room apart from your own. Here's a wallet. Till we meet again . . .'

Next morning when the limousine comes, I go to her room. It's empty except for the chest. I follow her instructions and go to the next town. The wallet's full of money. I place the chest in a separate room and hit the red-light district. When I get back it's two in the morning and I've spent the lot. I sit on the edge of my bed and groan. Suddenly, there's a rustle of skirts, and she's standing in front of me.

'I forgive you,' she says. 'Here's more. Keep away from booze and cards. And other women.'

I blink and she's gone.

In the next town, the wallet stays full, no matter how much I spend. One evening, however, I make the mistake of counting the money before going out. From then on, it begins to dwindle. I pick a fight and they drag me home cut to pieces. I wake with my body throbbing, aware someone's bandaged me. She's sitting beside my bed. I sit up, peel off my bandages and find my wounds have healed.

'My name is Lulu.'

'Lulu! Lulu! Lulu!'

I reach up for her. She comes into my arms. We make exorbitant love. From then on we travel together, the little chest on the seat opposite us. My lover's beautiful and rich. What more could a man desire? One morning, I wake to find she's gone again. As my instructions are to travel on, travel is what I do. I tell the chauffeur we'll leave at midnight. With the chest on the back seat next to me, we set off. After a while, I notice a glow coming from the little chest. I put my eye to a crack and see that inside there's a tiny room, elaborately furnished. A woman is pacing up and down. I can see she's pregnant. I fall back against my seat, my breath coming in gasps. It's my angel.

The chauffeur stops the car. 'Would you care for a cigar, sir?' he enquires, sliding back the glass panel.

At the next town, I carry the chest upstairs more carefully than I've ever done. Then I lie down on the bed and wait. Lulu enters very quietly.

'So now you know.'

'Well, at least you're back to the right size. How did you make yourself so small?'

'Do you still love me?'

She melts on my lips. My hands run under her blouse, finding her breasts, exploring the slender swelling of her tummy, the swoony slope of her buttocks . . .

'It can't hurt the child, can it?' says I.

'Promise you'll never say unkind things to me?'

'I promise. I promise.'

We travel on as before. One evening, I'm sitting between a couple of young women at a party, drinking a great deal of red wine. Lulu starts playing the guitar and everyone listens to her sing. That puts a stop to my flirting. When she's finished she gives me a loving smile and points with gentle reproof at the red wine I'm knocking back.

'Water's for midgets!' I exclaim, flinging out my arms. 'And so is music!'

A huge red stain spreads over the tablecloth. I realise what I've done.

She begins to play again: 'Let us spill a little more music,' she says.

I sleep on my own that night. Next day she tells me her song of the night before was a song of parting. 'You broke your promise. I have to say goodbye.'

'Listen,' I say, 'I'm sorry, OK? I'm sorry.'

'I am Princess Lulu Havitoff, daughter of King Lustigo Havitoff, King of the Little People. In my real form I am as small as the figure you saw in the little chest. Sometimes we little people take human shape and I have been sent here to find someone of a noble line with whom I could have a child and heir to our throne.'

'Well then, I must be the King of Egypt,' says I.

She nods: 'When I first met you, I saw at once you had royal blood.'

'Did you now? Royal blood, eh . . . ?'

Lulu's quite something. She really is.

'We change our size by means of this magic ring. When a little person of the royal line touches it, he or she grows to human size. Now I must use it to return home.'

We climb into the limousine. The chauffeur, sensing perhaps the end of lucrative and cushy employment, looks rather pissed off. The little chest is on the seat opposite. We drive into the country, climbing steadily towards the mountains, and the road grows steeper and wilder until the car can go no further. Directly ahead is a large cleft in the smooth face of a cliff. Lulu embraces me.

'Let me stay with you!' I cry. 'Please!'

'Are you willing to become as small as I am?'

'Yes!'

Immediately, she yanks off her golden ring and slips it on my little finger. I feel a violent pain and try to scream. We fall through the cleft, and I find myself next to blades of grass that are taller than I am. The ring has shrunk along with my finger. It's so tight, it feels like a wedding ring I've worn for years.

In front of us is a palace. It seems strangely familiar.

Then I realise it's exactly like the little chest we've been carrying around. We go in and find ourselves in the room I've seen previously through the crack in its wall. The entire court gathers about us, the King in the middle, inspecting me.

'Welcome to our kingdom. I've no doubt you'll make an excellent son-in-law. The wedding takes place tomorrow at four o'clock.'

'Oh, the wedding,' I say. 'Of course. The wedding.'

So there I am. A prince of the realm. I'm not unhappy, but I'm not happy either. Everything around me is exactly the right size, the glasses, the plates, even the cauliflower and the peas. My wife's little bottom is still exciting. She's shrunk, but I have too. So that's OK. However, I can't forget what I've once been. After a while, I start thinking of escape.

Early one morning, I wander away from the palace until I spot the cleft in the mountain. I try to pull the magic ring off my finger, but it's too tight. Suddenly huge raindrops splash down, threatening to drown me. I run under a stone for shelter and suddenly hear trumpets and shouts. The King's huntsmen are coming through the forest of grass. 'There he is!' they shout, and let loose their dogs.

I bash the ring – and my poor finger – against the stone until it bends – the ring, that is – then pull it off with a violent tug. I'm thrown back upwards through the cleft with terrific force.

So, here I am, larger than life, as they say. And this is my chauffeur.

'Care for a cigar, gents? It's the last box. When these are gone, there won't be any more.'

His face cracks in the simulacrum of a smile.

THE FIFTH REEL

'The primitive animal you went to bed with at night,' remarks Spider, 'was not the woman you woke up beside. Remember how you swirled across the dance floor with her? That eager sexual roughness was all you'd ever desired. No wonder you ripped the bed linen to pieces. Remember how she made abandoned love to you in the pedestrian tunnel under the river; how she rose, naked and beautiful, out of the stink of that subway; how you fucked like self-prostituting angels with the smell of rat urine in your nostrils and the cries of a thousand previous dank assignations trembling through your bones? It was indeed yourself clutching her, was it not? You couldn't believe it. You needed a witness. Someone who might apprise posterity of what lies beyond the dark margins of wisdom. Me.'

He clears his throat with an eructative rasp.

'Oh yes, I was there. I saw your besmirched feathers shine. It's the only place I know where the echoes die laughing. I mean, if she was truly yours, there'd be no limit to the Chinese tortures of assent she'd break you on. And if she wasn't, how long before all those crucifixions and resurrections she was going to put you through would make the religion of her cunt look very strange doctrine?'

He expectorates viciously.

'Either way, it was Easter. That's when she took you to the fairground, wasn't it? Remember how you rode the big wheel high up into the cool clear darkness above the lights? Remember how it stopped to let people off below? At the apogee of its slow turn, she simply leaned over, unzipped your fly, freed your springy member from the competitive privacy of those ludicrously skimpy sports briefs you wear, threw up her skirts, pulled off her undies and lowered herself into your cock. Now how was that for being plugged into several sorts of alarm at once? All you could do was stare at the pin holding your seat-cradle in the frame. She was rocking harder and harder and the whole contraption was tipping wildly backward and forward, clanking and screeching, and she was moaning to its screech, and you were deeper inside her than you'd ever been, but that pin holding the cradle in its frame seemed fragile, breakable, and she was becoming wilder and wilder, dismissing your anxiety with contempt, her hair streaming out, her hand across your mouth to stop you crying out in panic, as the whole cradle seemed to want to fly off into space. "Do it!" was all she'd ever say. "Now!" And you couldn't stop, of course, could you? That painful torrent of burning, exhausting depletion. It left you far behind, didn't it, a dwindling homuncule, like a man down on the ground waving at the last helicopter out? Your mortality boiled over into the

33

mortal afterflow and you vanished into the stars. Dear me. What an orgasm rodeo that was! And slowly the cradle came to rest and the wheel started down, and as you passed the people on the ground and the wheel began another upturn, you concluded the world was now your witness. But no. It was only me.'

With meditative force, he expels another silver blade of mucus, smack against the wall.

'She wasn't the woman whose good humour would casually leave the door open for the most intimate moments of mutual delight to wander in and out at will, was she? She'd simply kick it down. And what did you do? You just sat there like a ventriloquist's dummy framing the word: "kick". As for the primitive animal you glimpsed in the cinema, her ankles up on the seat in front, skirt drawn up, her mouth open, the projectionist's beam slinking sneakily between her thighs, her tongue curling upward toward that light-inflected tunnel . . .'

His voice has gone cloudy with catarrh.

'You could have gone into the movie business yourself. You could have filmed her not being the polite domestic creature the world takes her for. You could have become the world's most pornographic film director. Imagine: a pornography so explicit it would turn adults into children. Ha!'

'I'd like to have seen it, though,' he adds. 'The movie, I mean . . .'

PEDAL EXTREMITIES

I must describe Spider's foot.

It has six toes and is therefore of even proportions. Each nail is disfigured by a secretion which jissoms monthly behind the cuticle. The ends of the nails are disfigured and torn by Spider's lover, who cannot refrain from biting them when she is on heat, or has forgotten something.

The little toe, or bluey, has almost less musculature than Spider's earlobe, or Reedy Buttons' hard-to-find clitoris.

Behind the toes, the sole rises to a hump, which is a source of abysmal totemic love-energy. Spider's lover rubs her buttocks against it, smearing it with divine shit. Very slowly, Spider becomes priapic, like an old Victorian chimney.

'Reedy!' he flutes.

Then the foot curves in towards the instep, where the white flesh curls and crinkles, prematurely slug-like. If policemen run their pistol butts along it, Spider will tell all.

What the policemen do not know, of course, is that his words only appear to tell the truth. They resemble the world as it looks to policemen. In fact, they are verbal feet. They walk about aimlessly, crushing small insects. Spider giggles. He is powerless to stop them. The policemen are satisfied.

We come to the heel.

Occasionally, Spider wears women's shoes in order to expose himself to the sexual violence of repressed workmen on ladders. At other times, and in other moods, he wears a steel-capped shoe, equipped for faces. Now his lover takes his foot and rubs her cunt with his heel. It becomes slimy, wet, useless. He is Achilles, with wings for skidding on.

Ooh, says Spider.

As for the ankle . . . there's absolutely no point in discussing that.

A PORTRAIT OF
REEDY BUTTONS

Half turning to look at you, half wrapped in a towel.
An advertisement for bathroom furniture. Poised
on a ladder in a bathing-suit. An advertisement
for ladders. Or crouching in nothing more than
firelight on a rug. Very inviting. What particularly
solicits your eye, though, in the latter picture, is
the very special old glass of port in the foreground,
and the long, stretched-out legs belonging to the
male person in the background, who is actually
invisible except for his hand reaching for the glass.
Reedy is simply not there, although she is. The
presence of the leg-suggestive man, however, not
to mention the mighty glass of port, is voluminous.
The executives are delighted with this one. They
love it. So does Reedy. She's happy in her work.
Not only that, she's extremely fond of Spider. He's
her agent, naturally.

These portraits of Reedy – the ones you find
leafing through magazines in a waiting-room – constitute quite a portfolio of absence. But there's one
that's even more absent, which remains for ever
unpresented to your gaze. This portrait is elsewhere,
quietly going about its business. And you, going

about your business as you do, you're unlikely to let the possibility of its existence even occur to you. Why? Because it's only to be found in a simple wooden frame on the bedside cabinet of a very old woman dying in a hospice.

The old woman turns and reaches for it with an arthritic, mottled hand. She brings it close to her watery eyes and studies it. Reedy has gold highlights in her hair and a white ribbon. She has pale blue eyes, a straight nose and a perfect squiggle for a mouth. It's one of those portraits the corner shop does so well, and so cheaply, too. Your eighteenth year – measured in the simple phrase: 'Ready on Wednesday'. There's something so characterless about it, it leaves room for memories. For tears, perhaps. Yet the slightly blistered wooden frame is also a cage. A cage with solarised bars, through which a tiger alarmingly, yet somehow easily, jumps – although the old woman is completely unaware of this fact. She holds the picture close to her face, smoothing Reedy's hair with a tender finger, and as she does so the tiger prowls angrily, baring its teeth, licking its lips, clawing the bare wooden floor of the hospice, giving vent to snarls from time to time, resuming its prowling, becoming fainter and fainter as the old woman's erasing finger dabs at the picture, rubs at it with fondly obliterating strokes, so that only the suggestion of a prowl lingers in the room, a feline fetor, the vestige of a growl, something, anyway, that even the nurse notices entering the room to plump pillows, looking up and around, vaguely, and remarking:

'Could have sworn there was someone else in here, Mrs Buttons.'

LORCA'S HAT

On a windy Sunday morning after rain, along with youthful tramps, elderly foreigners, middle-aged dreamers, I visit the junk market.

I know my beloved is to be found somewhere, under a tower of chipped saucers, maybe, in the spoon drawer, among the stained ivory handles of ancient knives and forks, or nesting like a moth in the pockets of historical army trousers.

A young girl tries on Stendhal's ankle-length coat – the one he wore at Waterloo. The cavalry wheels about at full gallop. Hooves and horseshoes flash, the turf quivers under the squadron's weight.

Her smile, reflected back from the rusted silver of an old mirror, dazzles the riders. From far away, the thought of Lorca's hat reaches me.

Then she vanishes into the emptiness which smiles always create. I can hear thudding horses and cries of blinded men. The clash of cutlery is so loud it sounds like the nineteenth century breaking in half.

'Where is she?' I cry.

Spider shrugs. He's wearing a tanned horse-hide apron and a blue balaclava. Amazing what customers want, seeking the unseekable with the pertinent curiosity of vampires, looking for women, men, battles . . . All he can offer them is the past in the form of tarnished heirlooms, old lamps, brass monkeys, coins which would have bought the favours of anybody, oiled maps of victory with the spunk of rape still on them . . .

I try on Lorca's hat. Behind my reflection in the glass, I can see the remnants of the cavalry circling, blundering, lost . . .

'You pick it up, you pay for it,' says Spider.

To obliterate this commonplace odiosity, to summon the sweet, yet utterly unthinkable, I doff the hat to him. As I do so, the wind snatches it from my hand. Poems fly out from under it. Whirled up on a gust, both poems and hat float languidly down and become mirror-puddles for lethargic, ill-clad, shuffling feet.

'Five quid,' says Spider. 'You dropped it, you bought it.'

SPIDER'S LAST CASE

All the world is love. No? Well, it's worth mulling over.

Spider mulls. He mullocks, also. He garkles his penholders, blags a few desk drawers, druns a notebook or two and goolcocks a subordinate. These are just nervous gestures of distraction, much as you or I or Dr Watson would tamp a pipe or strike a match on a thumbnail.

Spider's thoughts have taken him far away from his beloved city. He's at yet another crime scene, with cruise ships hooting their exits from a port. There's a smell of weed and salt. Gulls cry between the chimney stacks.

The victim lies cruelly mutilated in the bilges of the hold, but the boat has a timetable to keep to, a thrumming shivers through the hull. From the bridge, Spider watches keenly as the sailors blag off the ropes, mullock the bowsers, garkle a bollard or two and then fall to goolcocking one another playfully. The SS Whoopsadaisy noses out into the slime.

He goes below decks to view the body. He might have known she wore a jewel in her clitoris, a chain through her right nipple, a small gold padlock on her anus. No wonder she filled ordinary sailors with disgruntlement, mere officers with tea. Spider resolves to track down withholding everywhere he finds it. First of all it will be the inexcusable transgression of women who fail to love sailors better than the world.

'My dear,' he murmurs across the great divide that divides them, 'I'd like you to describe the instrument that terminated your lovely career.' He gazes down at her. She is sprawled, naked, on a mountain of slag, which shifts, as the boat shifts, with the tide. His technique with a corpse is remarkable, intuitive and melismatic. Her eyes are closed and he riffles through her heart as if it were an ancient notebook. He leans back, concentrates with a frown, and in a vision he senses her reaching out slender coaldusty arms to him. He becomes chair-like and stealthy. It's not easy to prise open his tender side. Love's climaxes, he knows, are dark alleyways down which honest detectives may vanish, never to reappear. Anyway, the culprit is usually who you thought it would be. Unmaskings hold no surprises for someone as circumspect as Spider.

It seems the victim is about to speak. The beautiful underwater pouting of her mouth is shaping the name of her assailant. But he motions her to silence. It's time to go.

Spider! The last page! The whodunnit!

Too late. The moment a story threatens to unravel, he hates it. He always abandons plot. He much prefers the completely unrevealed mystery of the perfect crime.

HOW TO BE A POET IN FOUR EASY STANZAS

The street is cold as a good poem. The night is cloudless. Under a lamp, someone is standing in the deepest dip of the street, serenading a house front. This is poetry and it's me saying it's poetry because it is, although the recently slammed-down window of my lover's bedroom is a measure of just how the critical triumphs over the lyrical. Naturally my recitation is full of feeling. When the critics depart, the feeling is all that's left. Lights go on up and down the street, except for my sweetheart's firmly closed casement. My poem reaches into the black pocket of the night with a sneakthief's tender fingers. Her window creeps up again. Aha! I recommence:

> Cherish your lakes and islands,
> Weather, my lover, be kind!
> Harbour these recusant diamonds,
> The water and land of the mind.

'Cherish your own lakes and islands,' she says caustically. 'You'll wake the neighbours. Also, I'd like to know *who* exactly your lover is. Is it supposed to be me? It doesn't feel like me. Or is it the weather you love? Or is *she* the weather? No doubt *fickle* is the word you have in mind. And when did you last give me a diamond?'

But poetry is what I must do and this is me doing it, so there's nothing for it but to turn up the glitter:

> *Treasure the river, the pasture,*
> *As they gleamed before the fall –*
> *You turned your face at departure*
> *And put on farewell like a shawl.*

'Oh the *fall*!' says she. 'Do you mean the fall of man? Or is this some private, self-indulgent fall only you have experienced in the privacy of your hotel-like mind? And when did you last see me in a *shawl*?' How desperately I have tried to communicate a kind of tight-lipped radiance, and all she's worried about is her appearance! 'Haven't you got anything more melancholy?' she asks me. That sweet voice, husky with cigarettes. I stare up into her pale face at the casement. What shall I do to make it clear the melancholy fact of me saying poetry also, unfortunately, happens to be me?

> *My dear in your visions live kindly,*
> *In lovesmile and fragrance and act –*
> *Let your life shape itself finely*
> *On the wheel of a passionate fact:*

A silence. The moon has sailed up. 'I take it,' she says, 'there's more to come?'

'Yes,' I mutter. 'There's a fourth and final verse.'
She has no further comment and I feel encouraged.
At the far end of the street, I observe a man in a hat,
a blind man, carrying a cane, who is tapping his way
along the pavement towards me. I want to explain
to her how my rhymes constitute the language of a
parallel universe, where people are courteous and
exchange delicate aphorisms of the most intense
lyricism before floating away into a blissful fog; how
I doodle them out of my brain as naturally as plinking
and how this is me plinking them. But as the irregular
tapping of the blind man's cane becomes intrusively
louder, threatening to destroy my stanzas altogether,
I hasten to my conclusion:

> *These words were unburdened from me*
> *In a dream that no dream could be true.*
> *Whatever these heartcries decree,*
> *I give them, unhanded, to you . . .*

The blind man's cane whacks my ankles. 'I heard all
of that,' he says, 'from the top of the bloody street.
Unhanded? What does that mean?'

'Er . . . metaphorically . . .' I begin, half unwilling
to enter into a dispute with a disabled person.

'Don't give me no metaphor!' he cries. 'Can't
find my way with no metaphor!' He strikes the
pavement with his stick and sparks fly up. 'Can't
go nowhere if I can't hit it!' he cackles. Deep
pupil–less sockets, the weird blinklessness of unseeing
eyes, stare straight past me. 'See what I mean?' he

says and whacks my ankles again. I'd know that voice anywhere. And from the window above, my beloved calls:

'That's it, Grampa! Give him one for me!'

MERCURY, OLD THIEF

Spider has elevated the possession of other people's property into an aesthetic, and is acknowledged, therefore, by the rich and famous. Sipping sherry with lawyers in the Albany, he explains the turkey-fied dewlaps on his neck, the folds of loose carbuncular flesh on his gut, the bleeding swollen monstrous protuberance of his liver, that hangs, dripping, over his scrotum:

'On a diet of gold dust, oysters, virgins' lower lips, wild-boar truffles, plovers' eggs scented with spring garlic, the pizzles of young Highland cattle, the circumcised bits of female babies, how could I be otherwise than a man of enterprise?'

His health resounds in the bass energy of his cough. What Spider does not desire does not exist. He is a complete void who experiences the concentrated cunning of want. 'What will you steal, Spider?' they cry. 'Of what will you deprive the world?'

It's a gloved treasure. Take off the gloves and what do you get? An image of beauty without her gloves on, of course. OK, what else can you take off? Absolutely everything. But for the first stage of the perfect theft, the gloves must be off. What could be lovelier than gloveless smash and grab?

'You gotta steal it to know it,' explains Spider.

'Ahh!' say the lawyers.

In gestures, he describes his modus operandi. He performs a charade of setting out in a canoe to fish for it. He mimes the stroke of oars, the wee plash of the blades. A fizz of air bubbles rises from the floor of Lake Stupefaction. With a mulligatawny smile, Spider lowers a capacious, not to say illegal, net into the water, scoops up the treasure and with ratchet-like dexterity reels it in.

'What is it?' cry the lawyers, and bottom-up their sherry glasses in anticipation.

'What we have here,' says Spider, patiently unwinding a mummified sheet, 'is the drowned corpse of love.'

They peer like accident voyeurs over his shoulder.

Her face, to tell you the truth, is no longer there. But her teeth are perfect.

PHOTOFIT

He's shuffling the pictures on his desk. A mouth, cheeks, brown hair, the nape of a neck, jaw, eyes, the slim arch of eyebrows, forehead. A photofit, except it isn't, nothing will quite match up. Then he notices something, picks up the phone, dials: 'Goolcock, the ears!' he barks. 'Where are the ears?'

His subordinate thinks for a moment: 'Under the hair, sir, concealed under the long hair.'

Spider stares down at the jigsaw on his desk. 'You're right, Goolcock. I can see the lobe. Problem is, Goolcock, I've got a face here, but no body. Where's the body? No body, no crime, Goolcock. No crime, no investigation. No investigation, no need for men like us. No men like us, mayhem everywhere!'

'I believe if you look in the bottom drawer of your desk, sir, you'll find the body.'

'Ah! Just a moment!' Spider bends down and slides out the drawer. A sheaf of photographs of body parts is uppermost. 'This is no corpse,' barks Spider. 'When this was taken the woman was obviously alive. Taking a certain pleasure in being photographed, too.'

'That is correct, sir.'

'Well, if she's alive why are we looking for her?'

'Because we don't know where she is, sir.'

'Well, why don't we know where she is?'

'We have no forwarding address, sir.'

'For God's sake, Goolcock, what kind of investigation is this? You can't have the Metropolitan Police chasing after everyone for whom they have no forwarding address.'

'No, sir. Except in certain cases.'

'What cases, Goolcock?'

'Well, sir, is there not something special about this person, something that should not allow her to remain vanished? Study for a moment the sharp tip of her bosom, the long legs, the supremely straight back, her carriage. Do they not suggest, taken together, an aristocracy of the spirit, an inner royalty?'

Spider is a little taken aback. Can this really be the chubby subordinate in the downstairs office speaking?

Goolcock continues, his voice urgent: 'Should it not be the goal of all our purpose to recover this queenly missing person, sir, this kidnapped muse, this abducted flame? How else will the vision at the heart of good police work ever prevail if we do not recover the one who personifies, nay incarnates, the source of our inspiration?'

Spider is momentarily stunned: 'Umpf!' He leans back in his wooden swivel chair: 'What's all this stuff about inner royalty, Goolcock? She's got no clothes on. Is that what you mean?'

'As I see it, good policemen are in love with the truth, sir, which always goes naked. The missing person in question represents the object of our unrequited search.'

'Unrequited, eh?' Spider rubs the palm of his hand over the bristles of his beard: 'Seems to me, if what you say is true, we'll have to start tracking down all those girls on the top shelf at the newsagent's.'

'Begging your pardon, sir, but the ladies you have in mind are just crabs in a tub. Nothing very regal about a crab is there, sir. Nothing that would suggest a woman's power to transform herself into a sow, mare, bitch, vixen, she-ass, weasel, serpent, owl, she-wolf, tigress, mermaid or loathsome hag, is there?'

'Goolcock, what have you been drinking? We've got a mess on our hands here, and you're not helping any. We have a perfect confusion of heads, bodies, minds and legs here, a jigsaw-puzzle lady whose identity conundrum is wasting police time up and down the land, and it's got nothing to do with royalty, Goolcock, or crabs, or she-vixens, it's hormones getting uppity, that's what it is. It's a genetic travesty, if you really want to know. A genetic travesty!'

Spider slams down the receiver. Then he looks at the picture puzzle on his desktop and stirs it with a moistened index finger. After very long contemplation of each of the separate pictures, he fastens them together with Sellotape until a tall, naked, brown-haired woman stares intently back at him from the surface of his desk. A shudder steals up his body, from the base of his sacroiliac to the fine hairs sprouting from the ends of his nipples. He then carries her across the room and leans her against the wall. He sits staring at her as dusk falls, steps are heard in the corridor, lift bells ding gently, doors close, the building goes silent and night draws in. He remains motionless in his seat, transfixed. As the cleaners enter his room only on Fridays, and Goolcock is off to Tenerife on holiday, he will gather dust for days.

LIKE A GAME OF DRAUGHTS

I jot things furiously into a notebook, tearing the paper as I write. Three words only:

You . . . you . . . you . . .

Her amused rejoinder is that modern life is the fragrance of an original idea which is the source of everything that makes wrongness subtly enjoyable.

I'm holding the nib in a fist so cramped the knuckles bleed white. I know about the multitude of possibilities there are for a man like me. But in reality only one.

Coolly, she sits, smoking, in a wing-backed chair. Blue exhalations wreathe the outlines of her face, and sweep to the low table. Tobacco fumes caress the sides of a porcelain bowl and pour cloudily into its curved interior, stirring the dried flowers she has placed there.

Beyond the half-raised casement is the city. Strides of white sunlight jump the black buildings. She closes her eyes and removes the buildings one by one from her mind.

The word I've been scoring into paper has become mere slashes, leftward and rightward, a graph measuring adversarial fluctuations in blood pressure.

Her presence is a gleam. Silver in darkness. She

prowls the carpet in a reverie, commanding the dispositions of the game. The half-lit world of the room is where men and women check one another upon each square. A room where all alternatives must be considered. A room of endlessly played-out strategy. A room in which, one day, someone will die.

From the window, a burst of traffic noise. Squealing brakes. A crash, and shouts.

A voice – is it my own? – calls out triumphantly: '*You!*'

She gasps, turning towards the casement through which the dull light falls. Her blouse opens and shadows of clouds sweep across her breasts. She sinks back into the chair and the dark crevice of her sex fills with illusions and dreams.

Huffed.

THE CONTEST

Spider is judging babies.

'Dream no dreams for they will betray you, listen to no baby lies, no lullabies, take no comfort from your happy hiccups, for you gurgle in vain . . .'

He pats them on their chubby bottoms.

'Do you not see how serious and concentrated you look when you shit? From the gates of this abysmal playpen is but two steps to the cordial threshing-heat in which you were conceived. Can you not feel how a whetted blade concealed in clouds of nappy-lining hangs above us like a guillotine? Do you not feel already the rasp of the strong hand that will wring out your tears and hang out your soiled flesh to dry in the sun? If you bawl for lost friends, is it not true that a brute hand will thrust into your mouth something you would rather not have there and modify your behaviour yea even unto the electric generation?'

He kisses them gently on their chirpy mouths.

'Plant no trees for posterity, scribble no epitaphs for the departed, lean against no hallowed walls, travel no circuitous routes of amazing morality, but go there immediately with all the impurities of your heart.'

Spider makes love to their mothers.

'You may complain, yes, of this ribby sternum on

your breast, this harvesting mouth on your lips, these craving fingers at your body's ripeness, the plugged insignificance of the lewd and bludgeoning chorus I dope your ear with – but you must never forget the Women's Institute marmalade, the breeze in the canopies, Mrs Goolcock's meat pies, that look of incipient surrender in the vicar's eyes, garlands and bunting, the slow melting away of your fate into a pastoral smash-and-grab of the heart.'

They cry out as he forestalls their awakening desires.

'Peace, my wretched ones, your children are also of the earth, and were never born as innocent as this!'

RESURRECTION SPIDER

Only an actor, like Spider, really knows what it means to live.

I creep on to the set where they are erecting three tall cross-trees of wood. Spider sits watching them in a stained and dried-up goatskin. Next to him sits the swarthy idol of my dreams, Mary Contrary.

'I need the right kind of nails,' he says. 'They must be nails *this* big.' He grasps her curly brown hair and pushes her entire head beneath his goaty skirt. When I raise my eyes and see the traffic on the Laurel Avenue Expressway, I am reminded of the Via Dolorosa. Far above the multiple-purposed pullulation of the city, the ten-lane multi-level cross-and-counterflow with its stinking bumper-to-bumper tailback of thieves and executioners, an ancient biplane is trailing an airborne advertisement for Natty Bingwall's Bargain Basement.

'Suffer the meek to come unto me!' cries Spider. Mary is enjoying the nutty taste, creamy, not digestible in large quantities, of Spider's most intimate essence. Spider watches her gulp. As an actor he is often called upon to gulp. Good acting relies upon close obervation. He swallows hard.

'Jesus!' shrieks the director, Drabko Malevolic.

'Where's Jesus? He's needed on set!' And soon they have hoisted Spider up. The cameras close in, one to each wrist, one to his poor, eczema-plagued ankles.

People think it's easy being an actor, but it isn't. If you're an actor you don't know who you are any more. You know you aren't Jesus, but you look down at my white face and see me gazing up from the kneeling position, and then you think, well, perhaps I *am* Jesus. What a performance! I can see Spider's lips moving. I can hear his words.

'Give me back the boredom of youth, the mirror-sodden bars of silent sex failure, the anonymity of truth! Let me unwrap, once more, the chancy parcel of love. Give me back the energy, the wisdom, the ignorance!'

'That's not in the script!' yells Drabko Malevolic. 'Forsaken something Goddammit! Ely Ely llama sabbatical, for Chrissake get it right! Next take!'

I watch them driving laserbeam nails through Spider's wrists and feet. An arc lamp implodes softly, dimming the set. A microphone boom in the shape of a lance pricks his sides. 'Where were you, Dad, when I needed you?' he cries.

The President of Crucifixion Pictures winks knowingly at Todd Garbage, his assistant. He notes the pectorals in Mr Garbage's sweatshirt much as you or I would gulp oysters at a wedding. Drabko Malevolic, in a state of arousal, is yelping like a vivisected puppy. Spider gives one last scream. He has been fellated of his lifeblood by the glassy mouth of an Arriflex.

Next Monday they will not be able to find him.

He won't show up for any more scenes. They'll check all his known haunts – the railway station, the brothel, the corner shop on Roach Street. They'll search the echoing movie lot. They'll force open the door of his flat, but there'll be no one inside. We who sit in the darkened theatre know this. We're waiting for someone to rustle into the seat next to us, place a hand on our thigh, grin sideways at our ear.

We'll turn our heads and gaze into his shadowed eyes.

THE MYSTERY DEEPENS,
THICKENS, CONGEALS . . .

'It's a curious fact, Goolcock, have you not noticed, that the people concerned in this case are extremely protean? As in Proteus. One who changed shape often to avoid being questioned. Possibly a former King of Egypt. Are there any more of those ham sandwiches?

'We have the DNA. The photographs. The curriculum vitae. The diary entry for that fateful day in March when the oaks blew down. We have the testimony. The record of menaces. But that is all we have. The feeling seems to have vanished. How does one make an arrest without feeling? There is, it seems to me, a high degree of probability that we are not who we subjectively think we are. Who we are, Goolcock, is a matter for our unconscious, and the unconscious, of course, is quite beyond subjectivity – let alone objectivity. How should I, a senior plain-clothes officer of Her Majesty's Constabulary – for that is all I am – investigate anyone's unconscious? These sandwiches are abominable.

'We have the murder weapon, possibly. The solid ivory Benin love goddess, probably. The Aztec sacrificial dagger, perhaps. Occasionally we have, and sometimes do not have, a corpse. A corpse, more-over, who insists on proving herself not to be the person we think she is. Is anybody in this affair? As for the witnesses and other personages involved, they alter with bewildering speed, do they not? Imagine a tragedy being played for an audience in the fourth dimension. The characters would all be slightly ahead of, or behind themselves. The timing of cause and effect would be subtly misplaced, would it not, so that we, watching it in the third dimension, would feel . . . well . . . perplexed?

'Now lightning changes are something I know a little about, Goolcock. Before becoming a detective, it may surprise you to hear this, I was an actor. Indeed, I once appeared in a farce whose central joke was that by the end of the third act all the principal male characters had disguised themselves as vicars. Your father would have enjoyed it immensely. As a matter of fact, were it not for his mysterious disappearance, the Reverend Goolcock would be a prime suspect in this case. I'm sorry about this, but consider . . . Motive he had in plenty: a puritan dislike of hanky panky coupled with a longing for a more passionate relationship than the one he enjoyed with your mother. Means, he had also: Saturday afternoons were when he traditionally wrote his sermons, locking himself into his study. How easy it would have been to slip through the French windows, over the lawn, on to his Harley Davidson and into town! As for a weapon, it has not escaped my notice that there are any amount of conveniently blunt objects lying around in a church! Of course, Goolcock! Time and again, the old rule of thumb proves correct: the murderer is always someone close to us. He was certainly close to you, was he not? Are you listening?

'Consider the facts. Your father was a protean figure himself. You've told me – need I remind you? – how your father roamed the globe, sometimes with, but often without, a dog-collar. He was no stranger to silk suits and airports. No stranger, either, to a leather jacket and a pair of boots. Let's not beat about the bush. He also knew about lipstick, rouge, face creams, eye-liner, nail varnish, depilatory chemicals, sanitary towels . . . You told me about that cupboard. Oh yes, he was extremely well versed in the ins and outs of women's clothes! How easy it would have been for him to pretend to be our female victim and wait for the lover to arrive in the hope of having revealed to him, so to speak, from the other end, the true nature of passion! And then . . . Goolcock, this is amazing . . . by the most tragic irony of fate, it turns out he has chosen the very moment when the brown-haired woman, returning anxiously to her lover to make up for a bitter quarrel, finds none other than what is obviously a whore waiting in the apartment of the loved one. Thinking that he, or rather she, is a rival, she attacks your father. Fists, nails, high heels, what weapons are there in a woman's armoury? But from his handbag, your father draws a retractable crozier and smites her temple with it. She falls to the floor.

When he recovers himself, he assesses his position. He has blood on his hands. There's a dead woman on the floor. And he, Goolcock, is in drag. In my view that leaves a vicar only one option. A new identity and a ticket to South America. There you have it! Protean carelessness, followed by a terrible transformation followed by protean consequences. Wake up! We have work to do.'

A PORTRAIT IN ADAMIC
LANGUAGE OF THE BROWN-
HAIRED WOMAN

Fifil amarkalif palexli missagoolibash testobilli-o. Emna chapeen lessival appa dword. Chapeen ingalabbalo pindanxi fack reemli binlala binlulu shtoomp. Eenok eenok dazazar manetti fundaboo. Tootlab binleffi shonaganda arpastriss ma lizabono appa stenfadee. Heelipod doi tinfitwid looz lessival appa dword. Lestvo ingalabbalo ma chapeen atta fanoon. Eskorimo kollimop. Ta kipnabism tenfa kraieou appa dword. Amakoo shalowla! Fundaboo shillaba inalstropi!

Kreel akanastao lissop tschamka vag inspirax stepanoid ullurgalao. Pawsin wabbli lestvo appa dimp fack reemli. Fifil swang namstreep wup armalee chanchan invetiboid tinsamalinga lipsalummuk stenfapood. Fifil ganagon haali o heeli. Inastanog shimla pasnooli. Ohfijojo pandaquig appa dwendo palatina wao. Kraeiou shrapaeiou. Chuntli phuntli firkeemlibot zsarlapoon inspontimentakulus.

Seelabba fundaboo appa templatism. Yasmakao chiribabba toon vurgalaw kalastapeen oh-chi-phuntli. Chuntli kum-phuntli. Lizabono tipstanba matta lessival testobilli-o firkeemlibot sheemla rappaieou. Vag inspirax − chatta phuntli! − stepanoid ullurgalao.

Ollidrab ma kootsi fam fundaboo oh-chi-phuntli appa dword.

Kookafadookli.

66

LITTLE GLASS ANIMALS

From the balcony windows of my apartment at
Alarum Heights, I have a view over the city. A
platinum tower representing the wealth and power of
the Zukunftsmusik Corp. and Nostalgie de l'Avenir
Inc. (Paris, London & Oslo) has risen in place of the
cathedral they pulled down last month. Below me is
the Tuesday market. I firmly close the windows to
exclude the cries. Then I draw the curtains. At last!
In the gloom my furniture rides at anchor on the
carpet. A few slants of sunlight penetrate the curtains,
illuminating shafts of dust. The silence gives me the
illusion I have cast off. That I am sailing away.

A gargling street yodel persistently breaks the illusion. I walk to the window, throw open the curtains
and stare down. Directly underneath, I can see a man
with a pyramid of shelves wired to his body. His cry
reaches me quite distinctly:

'Luuuvvvleee glasswaaaaaaaare!'

I open the window.

'Bring that stuff upstairs,' I yell. 'I want to have a
look at it. Top floor.'

I watch him enter the front door of my building,
sink back on the divan, and imagine him swaying up
the stairs, clinking and clanking as he goes cautiously

round each bend in the staircase, making sure nothing falls off. There's a ring at the door. Those rotten teeth, that pencil-slash moustache, they seem only too familiar. Beneath his blue tradesman's coat, I can see patent-leather winklepicker shoes jutting like knives from the tight cuffs of his drainpipe trousers.

I examine his wares. Each little object has been carefully wired down to the wooden shelf on which it perches. Little glass animals, transparent and coloured. He points to them with pride: Anita Ant-eater, Barry Baboon, Carol Camel, Donald Donkey, Enid Eland, Freda Ferret, Golo Goat, Hedwig Hedge-hog, Irene Ibex, Jeremy Jerbil, Kiki Koala, Lemuel Lemming, Molly Mongrel, Nigel Nightjar, Oliver Ocelot, Patrick Panda, Quentin Quail, Rita Rabbit, Stanley Stoat, Tommy-Gun Toad, Una Unicorn, Vona Vole, Walter Wombat, Xena Xiphias, Yolanda Yak and Zelda Zebra.

'Any three for a fiver,' he suggests.

'Call these animals?' I cry. 'Where's the animal kingdom in this lot? What are these stupid colours you have painted nature in? And why are these animals grinning? Animals don't grin. Why do they have such stupid names? Is this supposed to be funny? Where's the soul of fear, cunning, and unselfconscious endurance every animal expresses through its very existence? Where's the skill and passion that should make life look as beautiful, terrifying and dangerous as it really is?' I give him a terrific shove in the direction of the open door, through which he stumbles, and goes off swearing.

Back at the window, I heave a flowerbox of dead geraniums out of its cast-iron socket and, when he reappears in the doorway below, hurl it downwards. It catches him on the shoulder, spins him round and sends him flying down the steps, smashing every single item of his derisory little zoo into multicoloured fragments.

Seized with the passion of my own mad stroke, I shout down: 'Make nature look real! More real! Seize its reality!'

A stupid thing to have done, I suppose. But have you never done anything stupid? What would life be like, if we had nothing to regret? And what does eternal damnation matter to someone who is able to discover, if only for a split second, an infinity of joy?

IDENTITY PARADE

We make love endlessly on the divan. He remains at his station under the lamppost below. The more vigorously we copulate, the more immobile he becomes. I use the word 'copulate' advisedly. Perhaps I should have been advised to use the expression 'pluto ace'. Between acts, I tiptoe to the curtain and peer down. He doesn't look up. A cigarillo dangles from his grey lips and a hat shades his features. We return to the task at hand. Propped on a lectern above her head is a copy of the *Anatomy of Melancholy*, which I read from while I pump up and down between the columns of her oatmeal arms. Whenever she sees I have reached the bottom of the right hand page by the fact that the expression on my face has lost its stern glare, she reaches up thoughtfully to turn a page for me. That's when I pause, lift myself off the bed, go to the window and peer out. I'm extremely glad to see that, little by little, he's getting smaller. The copy of the newspaper he's reading has shrunk to the size of a comic. His hat has dwindled to size four. His shoes were eleven, now they're eight. Maybe she's not the woman I really love. Maybe I am not the man she romances in her dreams. Love is a miracle broth of absence handed down from a heavenly charity canteen, and we're rowing frantically towards each other across the surface of a gigantic soup-plate. Our muscles ache, sweat pours off us, we're growing thin and strained like bolted cabbages. The words we whisper to each other contain secrets we do not seem to be able to unravel. Once again we perform the ritual. Once again I go to the window. Dawn is breaking and a wind is tearing shreds of dried flesh from a shrinking skeleton that is slowly crumpling in on itself, turning to a fine powder, leaving only the brim of a hat on the pavement. It feels as though we've almost reached a shore. A single sheet from his newspaper wafts up into the air on a current. I draw the curtains wide to let the light in. Then, with horror, I see the clock on the wall run backwards to three a.m. Night falls, the lamp comes on and there he is back to full size, reading the paper, smoking and not looking up. Her gaze meets mine as I turn back, and she murmurs tentatively:

> *you've never had a whore wowsy you*
> *with dark-mouthed, open-livered*
> *nightpiss sleepsex cheaptongue*
> *visionary philosophies . . . ?*
> *read on, read on*
> *across the dark of death, we'll meet*
> *there soon enough . . .*

FRONTLINE REPORTER

Staring into the landscape where an army is keeping its head down, Spider hopes to see, at any moment, the disconnected limbs of young men flying above yellow forsythia and white cherry blossom: the exhilarating springburst of nature captured in the gladsome exfoliation of land mine and mortar bomb. He's fearless. Doesn't want to miss a single crippling, evisceration or rape. Already he's off, brandishing his windshielded microphone like the softest of clubs, crossing into the war zone, capturing the human predicament at its loudest, his little spools turning. Springtime, lethargy, hot bullets, bomb-shocked fornication – the lineaments of scarified desire – he has to record it all, down to the last buried howl of 'Mam!'

Later, behind the lines, he sits at his dispatch table with a black patch over one eye, a walking stick not too far away. My gammy leg, he says, referring to an incident of extraordinary heroism and stupidity. People applaud his ridiculous amputee-ism. He plays back his recordings from the trenches. People are transfixed. Their skin prickles, their hairs rise. It sounds like, can it be, the gurgling sound of a bayonet administering the *coup de grâce*? 'War is beautiful, gentlemen,' says Spider, 'because it initiates the dreamt-of metallisation of the human body!' and he turns up the volume. Struggling to interpret a distinctly new kind of music, his listeners register plangent, slobbering sounds, hollow and wild and lost. Spider rolls his eyes and hisses in explanation: it's actually a new kind of love. What they are hearing is the clash of steel mask-snouts, as people attempt to kiss each other through a mustard gas attack. 'The metal Venus we shall worship in future,' cries Spider, 'will be an armour-plated goddess. Her symbol will be a ten-pound hammer bashing a lover's skull. As for Cupid's bow and arrow – what a miserably antiquated device! We can do better than that. No more love letters, gentlemen! Paragraphs from the heart constitute appeasement. Take your pleasures on the run and keep your heads down!' His voice crescendoes to a strident cackle: 'Love is war! The primordial art form! The only one which obeys the three unities in every respect and ends by putting out your lights for real!'

They make a note of this for afterwards.

When everyone's gone, he sits in contemplation, crushed by the light from his desk lamp, then reaches for a book of philosophy. Ah, the beautiful peace of incomprehensibility! His finger races over the page, his eye courses the print, his lips move, unfathomable explanations leap up and rearrange the night. There's a lunatic vivacity in his face.

Back home again, everybody wants to shake his steel hook. They want to see the half-inch of metal casing that was taken from his skull.

Spider will have none of it. He takes a train to Adlestrop and limps down a country road, listening to the twitchet of birds. He is enraged by a taxi that careers past him, fails to stop, and disappears round a bend having run over his artificial foot. The birds lack all conviction, and the taxi is full of passionate intensity.

'But nature is at peace,' I say soothingly. 'Listen. The fields . . .'

Spider stomps into the post office and soon the telegraph is clacking a message: *Must return to the battle zone soonest. Send light aircraft.*

I leave him standing there, scanning the calm of the sky for any indefinably small speck that might spoil the tranquil sheen of blue.

CHARACTERISATION OF THE AUTHOR AS A WORM

I'm standing barefooted in a night-time garden. The moon is up, a comet is moving across the sky, and the night air is pinching my nose like a familiar shoe pinching a well-known toe. One or two window blanks glow distantly orange. I can imagine the neighbours in their beds, punching their pillows with warm fury.

Time for what people like to call a worm's-eye view. I decide to survey the city from below, disguised as a soft-bodied invertebrate. My plan is to follow the exact flight plan of a depth-haunted desire. In order to procure an aerial prospect from the netherworld, I shall deepfly the underside of the building she lives in. When I get there, plutonic aceworm that I am, I will turn. I'll become a rebellious magnet in her memory, drawing her from wherever she is, out of bed, through the door, down the staircase, out into a garden just like this one, to occupy footprints exactly like my own, where she'll be vulnerable to my slithering attentions.

Pretty neat, eh?

I wriggle and insinuate myself into the soil, contracting and decontracting through the crumbly curtain that dissolves in front of me, skin-sensitive to the wet touch of loam, tasting the damp yeast of the environment I ingest and extrude behind me as I propel myself forward on the displacements of my own faecal weight, measuring, millimetre by tactile millimetre, the flight of my underground joy.

'Cree . . . eepy!' she murmurs.

My buried trajectory has brought me to the soles of her feet, which twist as she turns to look around. She doesn't quite understand the impulse that has brought her down into this garden. I'm as close to her as I'm close to you now. Now I perform another swift transformation, reach forward, and draw my fingers down her cheek. As I touch her soft warmth, my own skin flakes and falls away from the bone like paper tissue. She responds to the intense physical homage of my touch, becoming effortlessly real. And I disintegrate. The more tangibly she stands there, the more utterly I decay, becoming at last the wriggling arbiter of my own decomposition, feeding on my own riddled subsidence until nothing is left, and I'm lodged in the squirming interstices of her bare toes, where they are spread deliciously on the damp lawn.

Whoops.

I work my way back into the ground and float there, grumpily, on the clay thermal of my failed ambitions. It didn't all quite come out as planned. Everything about her was alive. She was a bit scared, perhaps, by what was happening, but she stood there like a female heroine. Me? I was just a squidgy annelid. Cold, damp, febrile. As for this melancholy relish I feel for the beat of my downward-driving heart, it's not healthy. I resolve to quit this underground mooching. Buck myself up. Stop loafing about. Best place of all is here in this garden, with trees and grass around me, a sky where stars fractiously glint and moonlight throws everything into blind relief. It's home, after all. Even if she's not here.

I'm back to human form again, you'll be pleased to note, standing on just the spot where her feet have left depressions in the dew-soaked grass. The tickling blades spear my Achilles' heels.

I'll just stand here awhile under the night sky.

And dream of worms.

SPIDER WORKS IT OUT

Detective Inspector Spider Rembrandt, gloomy investigator of stately-home interiors, knows exactly what he will find when he gets there. The dark oily coagulant of leftover blood. Someone has been up to no good. This is a capital crime, you understand, a really excellent bit of butchery. Goolcock is photographing two stone statues of Buddha on the entrance steps. Policemen with magnifying glasses scour the roof. In the velvet darkness of the hallway, two uniformed officers, on their hands and knees, are sweeping the black and white tiles of the floor with dustpans and brushes. Mrs Threedy, the housekeeper, fists on hips, is standing over them.

With a nod, Spider slides by them and enters the ransacked library, where the corpse is having her picture taken. It's not the body he'd hoped for, but it'll do. The police surgeon has replaced the limbs in roughly the position they were in before they were sawn off. The police photographer leaves and Spider closes the door quietly, inviting the corpse to reminisce. She smiles wanly: 'I was on the good ship *Lollipop*,' she says. 'It was 1949, the year I heard my first dirty joke. I met Arturo. He was the kind of man who would stand at the taffrail of countless moonlight cruises with his fingers under the bodices of seductive children, like myself. He had a way with him though. He could make you feel like the last vacant table in a crowded restaurant.'

'Quite so,' says Spider, his eyes glowing. 'What is a taffrail?'

'Arturo, my husband, was to me what a motor car is to a consumer,' she replies, ignoring his question. 'He sent me many glossy pamphlets describing himself. I was unable to resist.'

'One easy down payment?'

'All or nothing at all.'

Spider jots it down. An orderly recording of salient facts is the key to successful police work. The presence of a coal scuttle by the bed, for example. The hoofprint on an escritoire. His grizzled eyebrows twitch. Details always bring back memories. Memories of a previous time when comic-book villains, intelligently disguised as friends, betrayed the good with all the simple-hearted gusto of upturned buckets. Ah, the cruel present! Yet the considerate fashion in which her limbs have been reassembled on the Persian persuades him that little kindnesses can still happen . . .

'When did you discover he was The Claw?'

'How did you know?'

He points to the small leather suitcase by the desk. 'Always locked? But yesterday, for the first time, you opened it, did you not?'

'I didn't!' she cries, starting up from her chalkmarks. Then she bursts into tears. 'Oh I did!'

He waves her back into that curiously twisted and lifeless position with all the unflappability of a ghostly traffic policeman.

'And when you saw what you saw, you knew what you knew.'

Reflectively, he directs a jet of breath softener at his pharynx.

'Sometimes,' she sobs, 'I would get up at night and look down through the windows. Arturo would be busy gardening by floodlights. Of course, I had no idea . . .'

'Of course.'

'We never kept an au pair girl for long. Or a gardener's boy. Come to that, we were short of milkmen. There was never a lad to come and mend a fuse. Or at least, if there was, he only came once.'

'That would also have been true for Arturo.'

'Oh, but he was kind, thoughtful and gallant, Mr Spider! Even as he was sawing off my arms, I could see from the look in his eyes that he loved me!'

'And who is to say,' he murmurs softly, 'you did not enjoy the ultimate thrill of his homicidal attentions?'

It's all become clear to him now. How passionately disconnected human members placed in a suitcase to memorialise an unrepeatable moment proved too heavy a piece of luggage for her merely mortal brain. Flung far out to sea, a suitcase will always return on the tide. Spider puts two and two together. That warp in her husband's character. The tenement house in the docks, the room rented by the student. Slender, youthful Arturo, his trousers round his knees, his face buried in the aroma of used bedsheets, the cold teeth of truth burying themselves in his behind. All it takes is a moment of inattention in adolescence, and you're done for. If it's your destiny to come to know love with the persistent whine of a chainsaw in the background, how inevitable, later, that you should take on another identity, and become – your personable self turned inside out – an axe wielder like The Claw! Why does the past wish only to convey atrocities, catching up with us, out of breath, dripping with sweat, waving a telegram we certainly do not want to open?

'You won't tell anyone, Mr Spider, will you?'

'You have no need to worry,' he says, thinking of the urgent need to complete his memoirs before he forgets them. 'I shall certainly write a book describing how your husband, who had until that time harboured no murderous intentions towards you, was forced to use a chisel to protect his secret identity . . .' he winces . . . 'but I will of course change all the names. *The Wolf Flushed From Cover*. Would that make a good title, d'you think?'

'Bless you! Bless you!' The corpse is tear-stained with gratitude. But Spider has already gone . . .

He walks the unlighted streets of the city, his Stendhal coat flapping in the slipstream of pigeons, his flop-brimmed copper's daffer sitting back on his bald patch, age-old weariness of love-and-disaster ripples spreading around him, but his eyes bright with the kind of pain as one might, struck by a small stone in the testicles, be allowed by oneself to value, however momentarily, the sweetness of life, however short . . .

BUSKER

I walk along the street, stopping to contemplate a man in a shop doorway. He has a cap on the back of his head, and is strumming a guitar violently. His blue eyes stare from beneath grotesquely abundant eyebrows. His mouth hangs open, as if waiting for rain, any kind of refreshment. The whiteness of his teeth, however, is compromised by the degree of tilt they impart to his smile, revealing them to be cheap dentures. Although the energy of his musicianship is astonishing – probably worth twenty pence just for itself – there is one sad drawback to his performance.

He can't play a note.

Not only is the guitar not tuned, but the fingers of his left hand make no pretence of finding the frets. His right hand thwangs at the strings in a rhythmless, tuneless effigy of music, and though his body is bent in the ingratiated posture of the street musician who seeks reward for his efforts, it's quite clear, from the wild directionless gaze of his eyes, that he neither expects nor seeks any kind of contact with the shoppers who stream past him on the high street.

I stand in front of him for some time, wondering

what is going through his mind. I even hold out tenpence, but he takes no notice. It occurs to me that somewhere in his brain the idea of art must have taken hold, the idea of transformation, of grasping the ordinary, ghastly stuff of existence and making it into something else, poetry, music, perfect teeth . . .

While I stare at him, he continues arhythmically to strike his instrument, acknowledging neither me, nor anyone else. There's a kind of desperation about his strumming, a kind of finality, a curse almost. His jaw moves up and down as if, deep in some part of himself, he is singing, but no vocal sounds emerge. Then, for a moment, I'm distracted by something else happening. When I look back he's gone.

My eyes search the crowd, and I see him scuttling off down the street, released from my gaze. I notice he's wearing a leather bomber jacket with silver studs across the back, spelling out his name:

S ★ P ★ I ★ D ★ E ★ R

CALL IT NOSTALGIA

I awake with a compelling desire to revisit those parts of town where we had once been lovers. In particular, I want to visit the tavern where we had first declared our love for one another.

I hurry to catch the tube. Near the centre of the city, the train stops dead in a station and we are told to leave and go in an orderly fashion up to the surface.

As we go in packed ranks up the steps, men in firemen's uniforms, carrying axes and breathing equipment, come clattering down the stairs. Our pace grows a little quicker, and soon everyone is running. There are small scuffles, and cries of 'Oh!' as the elderly fall and are trampled on. Mothers snatch up their children. We come up into the daylight and I see an immense column of traffic standing still.

I haven't walked very far when there is a terrific, though distant, bang. Shortly after, one can hear sirens, and see helicopters chattering over. People get out of their cars and say things like: 'They've blown up the Palace! The Houses of Parliament! The Tower!'

I take a short cut, to get away from all the shouting

and speculation, and the stink of paralysed traffic. Finally, I reach the pub.

When I enter, I realise that nothing has changed. Everything is as it was. The same deep and serene quietness, the same malt-exuding dark oak, the same tender efficiency of the barman. Perhaps the floorboards are a little dirtier and darker, the chairs a bit wobblier, the smoke-stained ceiling somewhat browner than I remember. Two customers sit philosophically over a pint, not talking to one another. They might have been sitting there drinking the same pint for twenty years. I stand by the bar and find myself scrutinising the man behind it. I know that face. Only too well.

'Do you remember me?'

He shrugs.

'Nearly twenty years ago,' I say. 'You look thinner.'

'What'll it be, sir?' he says.

'You've even kept the same old barstools. Look. I sat here. She sat opposite me. Tall, with light brown hair. Don't think I didn't notice you noticing her. She was extremely vivacious, laughing and talking and smoking. You stopped serving the other customers to listen. Nobody talked sweet nonsense more reasonably than she did. It was an experience to listen to it . . . as light and intelligent as . . . as . . .' I try to find the word.

'As we are heavy?' suggests the barman.

I stare at him.

'You know, sir,' he says, 'I've never seen you

86

before in my life. In fact, I'd swear in front of a magistrate that you are the most completely unfamiliar person I've ever seen in this pub, and that's saying something. As far as I'm concerned you may as well have spent all your life in Borneo, till the morning you got off the ship and walked in here. But the lady in question . . . I remember her exactly. In fact, I remember the date and time as well. If you'd care to glance to the left, sir, just above you, you'll see that time has stood still since the moment I marked the place and left everything as it was.'

In wonderment, I raise my eyes and see a calendar, open to the month and the day of the year in question. It's a browned and stained page. Yet you can still read the neat pencilled marks. *Entered 12.15 approx, Left 2.26 exactly*.

With an expressionless face, he moves a wet rag in circles along the bar top.

PUNK SPIDER

Life is boring, so why not risk it?

His hair is raised in a solid cliff. It looks as if he's wearing a Roman helmet, or as if he has grown a scimitar across the centre line of his occiput. He's heavy with anti-jewellery: a chain is looped from his nose, he wears a belt of half-blunted razor blades, and his boots are those of a cruel stepfather. His clothes have been slashed to pieces.

As he stands and looks along the underground carriage, a wave of moral alarm breaks across the passengers' tired faces. Yet he is not really equipped for war: his stance expresses the paralysed gesture of someone who has swallowed the armistice along with the hostilities. He hangs suspended between love and hate in a paranoid truce. He is like the white flag of no surrender.

The train comes to a pig-squealing stop. We watch him from a safe distance, as he goes along the platform in a Braille of noise that we, hushed and respectful, can only read with agonised and over-tactile fingers.

Like a minotaur, he rises to the booking-hall on the escalator. He walks through the ticket inspector's gate without looking to right or left, without so much as handing in a ticket.

'Hey!'

He spins on a high heel and walks back. Stands. That gesture of humility combined with truculence. That studiedly dumb repudiation of facts, like an intellectual poring over a comic.

'Where's your ticket, man?'

'No ticket.'

'Gotta have a ticket, man.'

That recognition of a joke. Of a joke's web-like entanglement in things that may or may not be real. That smile of the man who sees beyond the joke.

Far beyond the joke, Spider can see his single-bed sitting-room in the still eye of a laughter storm. Sitting in a black rocking-chair, waiting for him, is Reedy. She sits in a ripped bodice, nothing else, next to an electric fire, sweating slightly. She looks like the mutilated victim of rape by newsflash photograph, her eyes focused on a horde of newsmen who have crashed through her door to find a potential victim who will not even pose.

'Getthefuckout,' she says.

Spider looks at the ticket collector as if to echo this. The Arabian colours of the bedspread wink at the luminous silver crescent moons on the ceiling. She taps her teeth with her pencil, opening her legs wider and wider. The newsmen back away, their flashbulbs popping. She has drawn eyes above the moustache of her pudenda. From the mouth of her vagina, she draws a balloon across the side

89

of her thigh in which she writes in capital letters:

This property is condemned!

The cameramen have snapped more than they bargained for. No editor will print this. It's not even rude. They restore the broken-hinged door apologetically to a leaning position as Spider turns and walks away from the regulations man. People run after him but their hands slither uselessly from his studded epaulettes and withdraw bleeding from his belt of razors. He strides along, clankily ascending the stairway to the sky above – a black silhouette mounting towards the irradiated violet of a late city sunset.

KEYNOTE SPEECH

'I died for beauty — but was scarce.'
Dominic Skyline

Spider marches out on to the platform to give an address to the World Punkfair Conference of Liberal Nightmare Simulation Morality Aesthetes. It's why he got dressed up, after all. His Iroquois haircut is ferocious. He has a serious message for the gladiators, and he delivers, believe me, a serious lecture, quite unlike the frivolities taking place in the bank next door. His theme is: Early Christian Sacrifice – Why the Lions Matter. His audience, though small, is huge.

'Listen, you pinheads,' he says.

A muscular thrill of anxiety-recognition fizzes along the spiky coiffures of the fourteenth-floor lecture theatre.

'The distinction between what you dado and what you dada is frankly such an odious fraud I propose to have nothing more dado dada with it. Stop throwing your tridents at me! Think of the world as an exit and myself as the swing doors. This is an emergency, my friends, and I'm locked! Think of yourselves as pretty young bisexual wisdom children descending from the heights of a multistorey car park and myself as a rapist in the ditch of the stairwell. Think of yourselves as a concept and myself as a high-up ledge. What are you listening to me for? Isn't there anything else on the radio? Wouldn't you rather get laid, you imbeciles? Wouldn't you rather throw yourself off? Or is it your dearest wish to be talked down gently by the Poetry Police?'

Wild uncomprehending applause breaks out. A robust Britannia figure, her spectacular breastplate glinting under the lights, holding a garden fork and wearing a fireman's yellow hat, crosses the stage, takes our guest lecturer by his freckled hand and draws him gently from the podium.

I, PUBLISHER

What is currently distributed by lorry to the provincial bookshops is a kind of dough that has been ingested by fog and evacuated by horses. How can this be? What dreadful transubstantiations are so-called authors attempting to pass off as 'real life'? I fear that what we are being served up with here is little more than a cracked jigsaw of skulls. All this fearful preoccupation with character. It isn't childhood that makes us what we are. Or failed romance. It's clean towels. Why should we have to put up with the eternal hairy mother figure? The only incestuous feelings I had as a child were for a lawnmower. I remember stroking the smooth curve of its rollers and trying to insert my childish penis into the crack between its blades. Fortunately it didn't spring to life.

You would not believe the amount of Gothic claptrap I am invited to read. As my authors do not send me works I wish to publish, I will have to do the job myself, though just thinking of the word 'novel' stirs up a squeaking among the mice on my desk. Why do people write as if man were good? There's no morality in that. Why do they write as if man were bad? There's no morality in that either. Man is neither good nor bad. He is not even somewhere in between. Where then can he have got to? Everything one reads is style, conversation, and observations you have already made for yourself. I long for the kind of book that begins to disembowel you on page five, in which you, the reader, turn out to be the murderer, and the last page is a noose.

My latest author arrives. His memoirs, he says. I offer him tea and express my polite optimism that one day mankind will stop remembering altogether. His observations on life, he says. My interest level succumbs to deep narcosis. Why did I ever bother to become a publisher?

'The world!' says Spider. 'Love! Crime! Passion!'

Actually, I doubt it. You can always rely on authors to direct a rheumy gaze at things just out of their reach. The sheets of their neatly typed effusions move across my desk like cockroaches. I read them and yet I do not read them. The focus of my brain seems to fall somewhere between their lugubrious periods and itself.

'Ah, the world,' I say. 'Well, there it is. Look through the window. Out there, as you can see, it's raining: a street full of drenched people waving hello and huddling under umbrellas. Criminals to a man, I've no doubt, and passionately in love besides. Your readers, I presume, waiting for your autograph? They do like to read about themselves, don't they? Twenty-five novels so far, is it? Twenty-five sandwich boards for you to pace up and down in?'

He has no idea what I'm talking about. He looks at me like a rain butt.

'This latest threnody,' I say, 'all six hundred pages of it . . . What's it really about? It's about itself. Pointless! I've never fathomed why the public needs to have its face held up to it in a book. No, no. If you must write something, why don't you do something different? Let it rain on your language. Expose your story to the downpour. Strip the rainwear off your characters. Push them out naked into the deluge. Hard to do in a mere book, I admit, but you could try.'

His jaw hangs like a broken stable door.

'Become a wet-weather nudist. Take off your clothes, walk out there into the car park and immerse yourself in the rain butt under the drainpipe. Don't try to surface when you feel yourself asphyxiating. Enjoy the element. Open your mouth and breathe in water. Feel it turn to oxygen in your gills.'

He is now – for him – concentrating quite hard.

'Don't climb out till you're ready. Amazing how different everything will look. The whole city will have turned into a pond with people sitting in rowing boats and unattractive rain-hats, fishing . . . It'll be water as far as the eye can see. Except for you, my friend. You'll be the stylish fin cruising between their lines. *You*, my hypocritical friend, *you* will be King Fish.'

His jaw closes with a snap. Hooked.

THE TALE OF THE PUBLISHER'S CLERK

The morning has begun with a painful interview with my boss. My work is slovenly, my dress sloppy, my breath atrocious, my proof-reading vile. A new edition of a great English morality tale has been rewritten in Adamic language. The story has become a monstrous labyrinth from which there is no exit but death. Not only that – somehow an edition of a much-loved children's book has become interleaved with a classic love story so that at one point a furious gardener, his spade raised, is seen to chase a willowy heroine through the lettuces. Abject boredom on my part? The typesetters, skylarking?

Or what?

I'm fired. I leave Dreadmool the publishers, descending through dingy floors piled high with forlorn typescripts, out through the glossy foyer where the only elegant person in the entire building is purring at a telephone. I show her my clawed features and step into the street. There has been a storm and the broken surface of a nearby alley is a wide puddle. In its black surface are reflected the tall chimneys of Neesden's Bone Mart.

'Jump!' hisses a voice behind me. It's an assassin, in

ponytail and beret. He's wearing a filthy assault jacket, combat trousers, and wields a Saracen's knife with a toothed blade. He bares foul teeth at me in something which isn't a grin. I jump, let me tell you.

It's a mad pursuit across busy thoroughfares, off and on buses, roller-skates, milk floats, electric tricycles for the handicapped, across parks and pedestrian precincts, in and out of public toilets, round kissing statues and packed museums, always that loping figure behind me, his bob-tailed hair glimpsed in shop-window reflections, his knife glinting in the sunshine, the air filling with cries and expostulations of those who can see what is happening and dare not intervene. Every ruse I try to shake him with, every decoy, dodge and double-back, loses him only for seconds, and then he pops up again. Soon, I realise the police have been tipped off and are following events closely, but not interfering in case I come to harm. I pray that on some rooftop a police marksman is even now lining up my tormentor in his sights. And as I run, I hear his voice intoning an endless and incomprehensible litany of accusation. I'd know that language anywhere. I invented it.

I feel safest in crowds. Broad street markets, for example, where stalls line the pavement and shoppers mill and jostle. No time for the soft exchange of pleasantries that might deter homicide. My pursuer, I know it, has just one purpose: to slither that knife of his into the pleasantly widening puncture of my skin. I hurtle past an old man loading a bunch of fresh nettles into a wicker basket, a cheery greengrocer handing a prickly pear to a toddler, skid on a slime of dead lettuce leaves and plunge into an arcade where huge black puddings and liver sausages hang like nightmares from the Victorian ironwork.

Perhaps my pursuer is an incarnation of that irate gardener, and I have become the bunny all the children love, the one who gets up to, well you know . . . Obviously the gardener is out to behead me with the guillotine edge of his heavy-duty spade. Can bunny escape? Will bunny ever see his mother again? Are not one's fundamental sympathies, perhaps, with the gardener? It's amazing the thoughts you have when you're running hard. Out of the covered market, over the road, through the scrollwork gates, I gasp my way across the greensward of the Regent's Gardens, realising, no, I've become the indolent, prick-teasing heroine of that English classic, galvanised into a sprint, and the gardener behind me, his boots crunching the herbaceous border, has other things on his mind than merely punishing a theft of lettuces. He's a gibbering cultural psychopath, one of the fiction-driven insane. What will he do if he catches me? It doesn't bear thinking about. Onward I run, over the Palladian grass of the park, thinking of my unfair dismissal, my lack of fitness. Damned if I'll comply with a madman's wishes. I'm simply too gorgeous to meet such an undignified end. The author who wrote me has no idea who I am. I'll show them all. I race out of the park and up the approach road to a famous hotel. Perhaps by whizzing around in the revolving doors, I can trap him long enough for the marksman on the rooftop to shoot him down. My long legs pound the asphalt. Policemen lining the route are applauding softly and I feel encouraged. I hurl myself at the swing doors and go round twice, hoping to catch a glimpse of him. The next thing I know, I'm sprawling on the pavement with a boot on my neck. Two policemen jerk me to my feet and march me towards a waiting van. Crowds have gathered. 'They've got him!' they call out. I struggle in the armlock of my two captors. There's a mirror on the side of the van, and I reach up with my hand to pat my brown hair. What the mirror gives back to me, however, is bad teeth, a crooked beret, a dirty, greying ponytail in a guerrilla riband. I wrest myself from the policemen's grasp and turn to look back towards the revolving doors of the hotel which are still spinning. Everyone else is looking that way too.

But I have vanished utterly.

ROLE PLAY

It's the weekend and Spider devises a simulation game he calls *The Universe at Gun Point*. In order to perform this epic pastime, he throws most of the furniture out of the window and draws a map of the world on the floor.

I call a psychiatrist.

When she arrives, I tell her I am a poet, formerly of Bristol. 'For many years,' she says, 'I was a doctor in Bristol, but the suicidal malevolence of the inhabitants, the endless plagues, etc . . .'

I look at her with the sympathy of the forgotten.

There's a ring at the doorbell and two undertakers enquire mistakenly after a body. Down below, in the courtyard, their funeral car is parked.

'The capacity of your hearse, boys,' says Spider, putting his head through the door, 'will not prove sufficient for what I have in mind.'

He has now positioned a tiddly-wink army for total conquest of the western carpet, and in the absence of any really cunning adversary seems set for the kind of victory that will make total war look like bluff. The undertakers have offered to play Spider for mastery of the known kitchen, bathroom and living-room. Not to mention the hall.

'Reminds me of Bristol,' observes the doctor. 'Can you hear gunfire?'

I tell her I have always refused to acknowledge the troops in the supermarket, the running gunmen in the streets. 'I am an intellectual,' I say. 'I simply ignore guns. I think guns are silly. I think people who play with guns are silly. Don't we have literature and art and all the wonderful world of the imagination to play with?'

'Often the cities we choose to live in seem like Bristol to many of us,' says the doctor. 'Look how baffled the patient seems. His inner turmoil seems to have encountered an outer turmoil as weighty as his own.'

And indeed the undertakers, employing time-honoured coffin-bearer strategems, have occupied several hitherto untrodden zones of carpet, their eye-brows raised to the *dignity-must-walk-in-the-strangest-places* position. Spider, whose game it is, wears the ravaged, beautiful face of a man whose finest inventions do not, ultimately, belong to him. Mr McMichael and Mr McPatrick, on their knees in their best weeping trousers, top hats tilted over their noses, are regrouping their panzer division in the loo for a thrust toward, the leg of the bed, which will cut off Spider's thimble cavalry and take the fortress represented by the gleaming porcelain of Spider's gazunda.★

I clear my throat, but the screams and dust of

★ Gazunda the bed

a battle in progress cause me to suggest a retreat to the kitchen. There's a pot of tea on the go. I drink deeply, remonstrating with time, history and sour milk. Beyond the net curtains I can see two hundred tower blocks, such as the one Spider lives in, and an army of scavengers traipsing up and down the outside staircases. I can see the faces of ordinary ill-to-do men and women like myself, noses pressed to the glass. I speculate that each lives in an apartment like this, with *The Game To End All Games* being played out behind their backs.

'I have often thought what it must be like for men of your sort who find they have to live with people like him . . .' here, with some disdain, the doctor points towards the room where Spider is, 'whom they have been deputed to care for, as it were, by a Supreme Being they have not met and would not care for if they did, let alone engage in a dialogue with that would make sense to either of them. It is as if . . .' and here she steals a handful of Spider's ginger biscuits, 'as if someone you don't know, someone with whom you've never had communication, someone, indeed, who actually doesn't exist, has put you in charge of a situation you'd rather not be. And, naturally, you can't very well ask him – it might of course also be a *her* – why you are not the person she thinks you should be. You see?'

I haven't a clue what she's talking about, but I nod terrifically. I tell her the faith in which I believe has, up till now, been utterly ignored; how you cannot have a faith unless there's more than one of you to have it, and would she like to join me? I tell her how I place my faith in metamorphosis and metaphor, and, unable to take my eyes off the tender swing, beneath a close-fit sweater, of her bristols, I jerk my thumb in the direction of the bedroom and suggest a little role play for ourselves. If she would like to play metamorphosis, I'll play metaphor. She looks at me blankly. No! No! My language has become beetle-browed! How shall I stop this slither? I pull a mental pin on the grenade of my ramblings, clamp it between my teeth, and count the seconds.

All this time she has been listening for something. A cry goes whooping up from elsewhere and she nods at me with deep psychiatric understanding. Somebody has won. In the confusion of my excitement, I hiccup and swallow the pin of my thought grenade. That's it. A horribly powerful brain-bang detonates my ego. My deepest convictions, my life-values, my lovely self-respect, all explode outwards in a disgusting shockwave that covers the carpet, the dado, the wainscot, the dada, the windows, everything.

Spider walks triumphantly through da door.

THE BEST CLUB IN TOWN

Out for a walk one evening, I become aware of him beside me in an impeccable double-breasted waistcoat, exhibition trousers, and a swallow-tail coat.

He invites me to his club and clicks his fingers in the air. Immediately, a limousine pulls up beside us and we sink into its leather seats. I take a Havana cigar from a diamond-studded cigar holder, a nip of elegiac liquor from a neat gold flask.

Entering the club, the first thing I notice is an orchestra of beautiful women, playing opulently vacuous music. At the tables, crowds of elegant people are drinking champagne from chiselled flutes. In their eyes, I can see a horrible glow, a fierce desire for something that isn't boredom. I can see rooms behind rooms, glittering with mirrors that reflect further rooms, all well equipped with the paraphernalia necessary for losing your shirt. Some of the clients already have.

'Are you hungry?' enquires Spider. 'Pelican hearts, perhaps? Or, if you'd prefer, a fricassée of unicorn tongues . . . ?'

'Albatross claws,' I say unhesitatingly.

'An excellent choice,' murmurs Spider. 'May I offer you, as accompaniment, a vegetable confit of prehistoric herbs, unfrosted from a unique location nearly a mile beneath the tundra in northern Greenland?'

We sit at a table on a little balcony high above the room. I eat heartily. My host, however, claiming he never feels the need, orders nothing. I can't help noticing how his eyes burn as he contemplates the goings-on around him. I compliment him on his chef. His body fattens like a flame at this, but he has no conversation. I venture some apophthegms on the theme of art and culture, but his reaction is just an indifferent nod of the head. I mention the word 'love' and he points dismissively at the acrobatics of some of the customers in the rooms behind us. We discuss the state of the world and his entire body crackles in a shower of fiery amusement. For a moment I think I've done him an injury. There's a distinct stench of sulphur. Perhaps his digestion is not in order? I move on to the ever-interesting topic of religion and the existence (or non-existence, naturally) of God. Tears of laughter spring to his reddened eyes, and his whole body shakes and throws off little sparkles of flame. People cry out in approval at this, though it's hard to say what they're approving of. I stare down at them, where they are acting out with redoubled energy some of the scenes depicted in the aroused canvases on the walls of the club.

'I suppose the old gentleman . . . ?' I murmur.

'. . . retired,' says Spider. 'It was all getting too much for him.'

Then he offers, as I guessed he would, to play

poker for my immortal soul and I lose it with as much regret as if it were a cancelled credit card. We retire to a lounge, sink into deep chairs, and cognac is brought. I stare up at the shimmering figure of the all-girl orchestra's conductor. She returns my look and adds a smile of deeply unnerving complicity. Her face is perfectly heart-shaped. I emit a terrific belch, which is amplified by some hidden microphone and broadcast all around the club. Many people, I notice, applaud my sally. I begin to feel obscurely pleased with myself. 'Those herbs are a powerful aphrodisiac,' I murmur.

'Urinate now,' commands Spider. 'Your orgasm will be more explosive.'

The sepulchral authority of his voice mesmerises me, and I walk to the men's room, my mind a blank scroll of physical anticipation. After relieving myself copiously, I push open the door to return to the club and find myself in a stinking alleyway of broken beer bottles and snoring beggars. Thinking I've made a mistake, I turn back and a brick wall confronts me. Well, well. Trust Spider.

I walk down the alley towards a main road. Opposite me is a giant placard. It depicts a pilot in the cockpit of his own personal jet, screaming downwards at Mach 2 towards the ground, a cigarette nonchalantly dangling from his teeth, a smile of welcome on his face. Underneath this rather dashing scenario are the words: *Bristols, Your Smoking Choice*. Too late to pull out of the dive now.

Then I hear the clack of high heels along the

pavement. It's the conductor of the all–girl orchestra. Her gaze catches mine with a prolonged and tender yearning, but with a shiver I realise her power of conduction has gone. She's old. The wrinkles round her eyes are scored deep. The lines in her face have pulled the heart shape of her countenance into a falling arrowhead of failure and regret. Her dress, so alluring, so glittering under the lights, is just a stained and shabby frock. I say nothing.

The empty street echoes with the clip of her departing heels.

PHILOSOPHICAL SPIDER

Doctor Julius 'Spider' Rembrandt settles between the wings of his buffalo-hide armchair, places his ostrich-calf boots on the naked posterior of a kneeling boy, adjusts his pince-nez and delivers himself of some barbed *aperçus* on the subject of contemporary society. His assistant, the delectable Reedy Buttons, records his utterances using a felt-tip pen across the creamy back of a former railway *danseuse*, who stands with her face to the wall in order to act as a human blackboard. In this fashion, work continues through the morning until the young lady's shapely back and legs are closely covered with neat jottings, crossings-out, algebraical formula, and phonetically rendered expostulations of indescribable loneliness. Then Dr Rembrandt's housekeeper sounds the bell for lunch somewhere in the bowels of the house and Spider swings his boots to the soft carpet and strides to the blackboard, re-reading his work. When he has finished, Reedy Buttons, with a practised movement of her braceleted wrist, unbuttons the flap in his pepper-and-salt plus-fours, allowing his virile member to extrude. He parts the young lady's trembling hindquarters with firm, doctorly fingers, so that he can read the last sentence which Reedy, with skill born of long presumption, has contrived to write in such a way that the young lady's anus forms its full stop. Remarking crisply that the only way to investigate the true meaning of an utterance is to penetrate the predicate to the full, Dr Rembrandt, employing a technique he has learned at the Cairo Institute for Divination and Perfloration, gently eases his sightless discoverer into the young lady's tiny rosebud eye, sinking ever deeper into that illuminated garden from which no one ever returns blind. As Dr Rembrandt engages in repeated strokes of philosophical connection with error, deeply excited to find that plumbed fraudulence surrenders intimate vestiges of truth, he is rhythmically accompanied by the snapping sound of Reedy Buttons' middle and index finger against a new one-hundred-pound note which she holds up to the young lady's gaze. There follows a long deep moaning exhalation, as of one expelling some kind of demon. Dr Rembrandt takes a pace back and buttons himself up. 'I think I understand now,' he says, 'what it was I have been trying all morning to express.' He takes the young lady by her shoulders and bestows a kiss of appreciation on her lips and breasts. Genially, he gestures to the youth, who is still kneeling on the carpet. 'The advancement of science,' he says, 'depends on inspiration. Nothing more nor less. Shall we go down?'

DEATH OF THE AUTHOR

The bongo player is a man called Cuba Johnson. His knuckles flutter against the skin of the drum. Outside, in the car park of the Havana Club, a man in a silver Coronado Orgasm de luxe Astrocruiser yawns hugely. He's been waiting years for someone to leave. He hopes he will recognise the moment it happens.

Entering an office to the rear of the club, a brown-haired woman takes a pistol from her handbag and fires once.

Two blocks away is a three-storeyed brick house. In the glass panels of its front door is a mosaic of St George rescuing the virgin from the dragon. The lamplight makes its dark colours glow. A man in a hat pushes open the door and begins to climb the stair. Softly, he ascends to the first landing, stabbing a blunt thumb against the bell of the first apartment. Deep inside, an answering reverberation forsakenly echoes. Spider tips back his hat, takes out a picklock, and opens the door.

Back at the Havana, the author lies sprawled across his desk. There's a neat hole in his temple, and blood is oozing from it. His cheek is laid upon an open copy of *The Joy of Imagination*.

The brown-haired woman tucks away her pistol,

clips a Groucho Marx moustache and glasses to her nose, and leaves the club with a vigorous stride. She walks past the man in the Coronado convertible, climbs into a 1977 model Volkswagen Beetle (duck-coloured) and roars off with the characteristic splintering-of-small-metal-pellets noise that the air-cooled rear-engine Volkswagen makes when being accelerated hard.

The man in the convertible is fast asleep.

Well, that's the story so far. Spider tilts his hat and clicks the door of the apartment shut behind him. It's like a hothouse, where the heating boilers have been left running for decades. There's a murmur, a crepitation, a humming, a fluttering, a flying, a zooming, a buzzing, a crescendo. Millions of small roused insects bump and zither in a cloud round his head. He shoots out thousands of silver filaments and fashions a crystalline network of infinitesimal ropes. The flies hurl themselves at it, adhere, flutter and die. The hothouse heating system belches and gurgles. Through the air wafts a warm hint of nobility fouled. On the mantelpiece, there's a portrait of the author, cheek to cheek with a brown-haired woman. Spider picks it up and gazes at it. Removing the picture from its frame and taking out a pair of manicure scissors, he snips round the woman's features, leaving a hole. Only the author's strangely exposed smile is left. 'One for you, old horse,' murmurs Spider. He lays the frame face downward, turns and walks to the door.

As he goes down the staircase, his body begins to

enlarge like an approaching black hole. His hat is the roof of the apartment house. His advancing shadow becomes the walls, the very fabric of the building. He *is* the building. The streetlight's beam illuminates an image of St George, the dragon and the maiden, in the door of his chest. The about-to-suffer-bestial-abuse girl is holding the back of her wrist to her forehead. Her face wears a look of alarmed coquetry. The dragon's teeth parody a grin. St George, who has tripped and impaled himself on his own lance, is expiring anonymously like an unknown soldier, his visor clanged shut, in the dark and mortal abyss of this final sentence.

NOT SO FINAL AFTER ALL

As a rescue worker of the real, I begin to feel these bits of writing need a little life injecting into them. Perhaps they will then inject a little life into me. What better, therefore, than a leisurely promenade through the drizzle? It's a pluvial stroll I'm advocating. Keep an eye out for umbrellas. Your jellies are likely to be dashed out by countless small women who are full of an irritable urge to go somewhere. Meanwhile, I resemble doubt's sister. There'll be no characters in this stroll; no one is planning to kill anyone or steal any towels. There's not even going to be any sex. It's merely raining, and there's an end to it.

(Talking of sex, I visited my imaginary lover a while ago, and I can barely convey the inexpressible delight it gave her to see me when I had the galoshes on. Boots and a hat. You know the drill.)

Very well, then. Like some kind of luminous crow I hop down the street. The rain drives in my face, but with my Torrential Downpour Aquatic Mk III on I'm happy. It's blissful when she turns her face to me, for she loves me, and it's a deep requital to be so completely misunderstood. My soul goes out to her as I walk in the rain. She holds me in her slim, naked arms and no one should underestimate the voltage that can run through someone who has been jumping up and down in a puddle. 'When did you last do that?' laughs the executioner, using his backside to put an edge on his blade.

O Venus.

There's been an explosion, but I think we should ignore it. What people want is trembling kisses, beautiful envelopes full of money. Life promises so much, yet there's always a Spider, isn't there, trapped in a coal mine?

He groans. He has found a copy of Marcel Proust, the only reading matter allowed in a miner's knapsack by the mining company. 'Shorter sentences!' he pleads. They debate the issue. '*Finnegans Wake*?' someone suggests. There is general hilarity. Spider's curses are awful. He needs water.

Of that we have plenty. I walk on as it swirls about me, inventing interesting characters. Probably I look rather like Marcel Proust. I invent, for example, Howard Plugg. With all this rain, the world is beginning to take on the aspect of a filling bathtub, so I keep Howard on the end of a chain to be held by the reader. In relation to my masterpiece, it will be the reader's role to play Howard's mother and jerk him out of the hole whenever the poem appears on the verge of overflowing.

'For Christ's sake!' yells Spider.

A vision of a man in, shall we say, *extremis*? His mouth is full of coaldust, he is dying, practically dead, yet his attitude to the company is one of supine gratitude. I love him. I pity him. He's a miserable worm.

'I'm dirty,' cries Spider. 'I'm dying!'

'Whereas I am exploring the possibilities of metaphor,' I reprove him gently. 'Were Howard not sitting with his bum over the plughole, the fullness of this poem would ebb away. And then where would we be? Not only would you not be down a coal mine, I would not be able to consider ways and means of rescuing you.'

'Call this reality?' shrieks Spider. 'What kind of writer are you?'

Well now. A challenge, indeed. It's a peculiar literature that has its characters remonstrating with their author, is it not? I ask Spider if he would like to negotiate with Howard, seeing as his behind is so fortuitously lodged over that plughole.

Naturally, he won't listen. Somehow or other, what began as a pleasant amble through spring rain has turned into a desperate bid for survival by a man trapped in a scuttle full of coal.

On street corners, they are selling *Great Disasters of the Twentieth Century* in the waterproof, bathroom edition. Spider is beside himself. Nothing will stop the ceaseless tapping of his bent spoon. He just goes on and on beating out morse code S.O.S. messages. More chipped enamel. As a writer, with a natural curiosity about the world, I suppose it ought to be my job to find out why he's telling me all this.

O drainage!

He should have had the sense not to go down there in the first place.

TO THE LIBIDO!

Torches high! Into the mouth, along the tongue's centre line, and down the throat! In front of you, ladies and gentlemen, are the pillars of the larynx. Magnificent, aren't they? Squeeze through, that's it. Loads of room! Now off we go down the gristly chute of the trachea – exhilarating, isn't it? – PLOP! into the pool of the lungs! Can't swim? Nonsense! Look at those crocodiles . . . ! See what I mean, of course you can swim! No, no they're not really crocodiles. They're words. WORDS. See this one here? Just a little half-suggestion of a word that never got spoken. Can't hurt you. Never did any harm to anyone. There now. Give it a pat on its rusty old nose. *Antidisestablishmentarianism*. That's right! Give its tail a shake! Alright, out of the water everybody, we're going to squeeze through the red wall in front of us into the dark chamber next door. Hear that antediluvian pump beating? Amazing, isn't it? This is the engine room. See all the rejected words on the floor? Looks like metal bladderwrack, doesn't it? Yes, missus, rejected words. Grab a couple and wear them round your neck, they might bring you luck. Now then, what we have to do is go steadily down this mine shaft. Yes. You're absolutely right. This is where the old fonts are stored. Car-wash Delirium. Tadpole Gothic. Simplicity Illustrated – they're all here. Lower case. Upper case. It's a labyrinth, ladies and gentlemen, don't have a funny spell in here, the paramedics will never find us. Lucky you've got me as a guide. Fifty-eight years on this job and there isn't a word I haven't climbed over, abseiled down, or cramponed up. I know them all. Where did they come from? How did they all get piled up into boulder heaps like this? Scientists have been asking this for years. Don't worry about it, over you go. That's the way, we're nearly there. Close your eyes everybody! Now open them! This is it: the round chamber. Wonderful, eh? That round stone, ladies and gentlemen, is the libido, completely circular and smooth, no way in, up, under, out or even – funnily enough – round it. Well, sir, beyond the libido – that's where it gets really interesting and the only way to get beyond it is through it. I knew you'd ask me that. Ladies and gentlemen, the only way through the libido is to think of a word you really shouldn't think of. Know what I'm talking about? One of *those* words. If you don't know any words like that, I'll whisper one in your ear. Don't roll your eyes at me, missus, that's what words like that mean. OK? You're going to jump straight into the libido. I know it's solid rock, but if you shout the word as you jump, it'll just open up and you'll be inside. If you haven't, it'll knock you out. Give a really big yell as you push off, it helps. Ready? Steady! Go! Mmm. That leaves just you and me, doesn't it? See that old sign. *EXTREMELY HAZARDOUS BEYOND THIS POINT*. Hardly any wonder they left it upside down. Well, don't worry, they're exaggerating. Let me put it back the right way up. Give the next lot something to think about while they're blundering around like a set of drunken explorers looking for the famous falls. Hold tight! You ready?

Jump!

SPIDER'S TESTIMONY REGARDING THE CARNAL KNOWLEDGE

It's like this, your worship: The boulder blocking the entrance to the cave rolls away at a touch. I enter with curiosity and no fear, though I do have anxiety, milud, as to what I might find there. My bare feet tingle. There's a warm and pleasant temperature. I half expect to meet dislodged bats, but apart from a pleasant slooshing, your worship, there's nothing. If the court will allow me to explain: I'm in a vault of ancient forms, lubricated by a constantly replenished torrent that runs in glistening swathes and ... well ... slooshes, your worship, I can't explain it better than that. But the air is clean and sweet, your honour. I'm a kind of cave painter. I've got nothing but a single primitive brush tipped with silver paint, with which, milud, I begin to believe I can capture the whole of the natural world. All it takes is a single recidivist click of my brain, and I can move among the gracile kingdom of the animals as freely as they move among themselves, learning their secrets and trapping them in mid-leap. So to speak. Yes, milud. Yes, recidivist *was* the word I used. You can learn your artistry from the animals, you know. You can fill great prairies with herds just by moving your brush. You've just got to learn how. Once you've got everything rippling and slooshing, your worship, you can ripple and sloosh along with it. Exactly. I mean, this is a total contradiction of the idea that a mere cave is just an empty place, rather dark, where absolutely nothing at all happens till someone like me comes along.

You may stand down.

AFTER LONG DRIVING

I have been travelling alone. My shoulders are stiff with the strain of concentration. For hours, the motorway has unfolded in front of me, throwing sharp pinpricks of light against my eyes. My head throbs from following night curves through uninterrupted rain. I leave the main highway and drive across a dark landscape to a market town on the edge of the map. In the blank hotel I gaze at the ceiling. I cannot sleep. My blood vibrates with the terror of me.

Leaving the room, I walk the street. It has stopped raining but the night is pervaded with a damp mist. A gang of youths talks low between motorbikes and chopped-down cars. I turn into another street and walk beside the loaf-like outline of a church. Coming towards me is Spider. He takes my arm. 'You wander at night?' he asks. 'It's raining, yes? So you walk.'

He sounds like a foreigner to me.

'It's the air that's foreign tonight,' he says gently. 'There are no sleeping-pills to rival lamps and fog. Wouldn't you agree?'

He guides me to a lattice gate in the fence around the church. It admits us like a woman's sex opening to her lover. We are in a field full of spirits, gleaming, flitting and vanishing. Candles enclosed in small lanterns burn against the rain. I have driven across entire continents to reach her, but now fatigue has invaded the marrow of my bones. I would have kept on driving, but a vision of death prevented me. Spider exhales the long shuddering breath of delight that is the mark of a cemetery fanatic. 'This is where they keep the corpses,' he says. 'Neater in death than life, wouldn't you say? Look. More of them.' And indeed, with their ears pricked, they lie, one next to the other, listening to our steps above their heads.

'This one had two wives. I conjecture he wore moustaches.'

He wore moustaches?

'My friend,' says Spider, 'the rain is all the moustaches you will ever need. Later you will remember your long driving through a downpour. How the ten-car pile-up across both northbound and southbound lanes heralded your death. How you drove past, your face glowing and flickering in the lights of rescue workers. How you looked at twisted metal and saw the white face of a child in a puddle of oil and rain. How you drove on, crying out silently against fate. And you left the highway, and came to this small hotel in a provincial town full of the voices of strangers. Look at this marble. These flowers. How perfect it all is, perfect as those beneath our feet are rendered even more perfect by these tablets of stone. Listen to the cars full of youths, leaving town. Your ghost will live on here in this marketplace, lurking near the cross, gossiping confidentially in doorways, reading these inscriptions, seething with tenderness.'

I'd quite like to go.

'But you will persist, my friend. In a churchyard of figments, you will persist. What else can you do, but listen to the endless howl of the traffic, murderous across the viaduct, and drift here, wakeful, untethered to sleep or logic?'

What else?

MODEL T SPIDER

Spider sits in front of his computer. Men from the motor trade cluster round his work station. They are interested in the methods he uses to design cars that ought to have been designed but weren't. Such boldness with history makes them feel flushed and sexy under their linen crinkle suits.

'The failure at the heart of early post-war British automobile technology,' he says, 'was to overlook girls. See how easy it is to persuade a girl to undress, transfer her receptive image to a computer screen, and then, gentlemen, after a short period of gestatory sleekness, in which the girl grows demonstrably more charming, to produce a perfectly human symbionic automotive replica product like this . . .'

The salesmen stare transfixed as an improbable motor car appears on the screen.

'Odd!' cry the salesmen. 'It's odd!'

'Merely a testimony to the complexity of the human sexual response,' he remarks, gravely. 'Gentlemen, I give you the *Ford Britannia*!'

He smiles.

'I think you'll agree that a motor car assembled with fully interlocking components of this type would have ensured a level of customer fidelity unprecedented in the history of marketing.'

'*Jesus Christ!*' says a salesman. 'We might still be driving 'em!'

'This is a motor car that could have taken over the world.' Spider mozarts the keyboard. Japan appears. Its entire road system reveals an accumulating traffic jam of Ford Britannias. The greatest download of automobile arousal in the history of pressed-tin sexual suggestion takes a mere twenty-five minutes to reach full erectility.

He ejects the diskette from the computer drive. It reads: *Nippon. Property of S. Rembrandt Esq.*

All sigh.

'Just a demo,' says Spider. 'Is there anything else in the recent past you'd like me to redesign? Your lives, perhaps?' He laughs satanically.

Looking around at each other wildly, the salesmen start to express love for one another. Despite themselves, they fall to the floor, embracing, stroking each other's wounds, and moaning like trains at night waiting outside stations.

'But it's just a demo!' cries a single non-participant salesman. 'It's just a demo!'

Spider contemplates them with disgust. He rises and walks to the exit. In the rainy street, parked by the kerb, under the shadow of a power-station wall, is a 1946 model Ford Britannia. A girl, dressed in a tightly fitting costume of black upholstery leather, is waiting for him. She wears a sliding-roof hat with a windscreen-wiper veil, throwing an intricate lattice-work of shadow over her *film noir* beauty.

She looks up as he gets in. He turns on the ignition. He pulls the starter. The engine turns over.

It fails to start.

All Ford Britannias failed to start.

Then. As now.

'I told you not to buy a Britannia,' says Reedy. 'What we need is a horse.'

THE LATENESS OF THE HOUR

In the infinitely expanding rush of the universe we are brief, individual hesitations in the otherwise seamless flow. This thought accompanies me as I ride a number one bus through dark city streets. From a cosmic point of view I am motionless, even as the double-decker careens down narrow streets and swoops, judderingly, around particularly tight corners.

A computerised voice announces the name of the next stop. When we halt, I look down from the upper deck where I am sitting alone. A number of shadows disembark and are swallowed by their own dispersal. A single shadow boards the bus, but nobody comes up the noisy stairs. Then we're moving again. The black silver of the window returns my face to me, a pale mask. As the thick foliage of the summer trees whips the roof of the bus, my face flashes its print through the stirred somnolence of the leaves.

The computerised voice enunciates something. Not a stop but a woman's name. The bus is halted, ticking over. Looking down, I can see under the lamp the tall figure of a young woman, waiting. She does not move. Then the bus driver's own voice reverberates raucously through the bus, reminding me this is the stop I'd asked for. I get up and go down the stairs. The pneumatic double doors of the bus stand wide open to the rainy, windswept evening. She's standing a little out of the light. All the passengers' faces on the lower deck are trained on me with petulant scrutiny. Why don't I get off the bus and let them carry on with their own journeys for ever?

Why don't I?

IN THE BEGINNING WAS
THE WORD

Spider has become an amateur photographer. He buys shiny magazines, piles of black optical equipment. Money is no object. He spends Reedy's money as well. Then he asks her to remove her clothes, and assume a posture, face down upon the bed, her glum chin propped upon her elbows, the Titianheavy loveliness of her arse quivering in the air,

'Smile!' he commands.

'How can I smile like this?' demands Reedy Buttons. 'I feel idiotic.'

'Show fealty then!'

'This is incredibly boring. What's fealty?'

Resigned to the whims of man, and with ironical exaggerated slowness, Reedy waggles her bum in the air. She looks like a seal falling off a rock.

'Fealty!' cries Spider, 'means you are the subject of my photograph and must say so. Go on, declare your fealty!'

'Eh?' says Reedy.

'Say after me: My liege, my lord, to you I owe allegiance.'

'I can't say that. It's too complicated.'

'But it's simple! Allegiance is the feeling you have

when the lens tickles your privacy and you feel fealty. Fealty is feely. It's the feely-faithful portrait of you at the exact moment when you are who you say you are.'

'Well, who am I?' she asks, bewildered.

'You,' says Spider, with the patience of an axe-maniac, 'are Reedy Buttons. Not anybody's Reedy Buttons, but *my* Reedy Buttons. By capturing each trembling invitation of your behind, I make you more Reedy Buttons than you've ever been. And because I insist so photographically on you being you . . .' his logic is developing the peculiar trajectory of a blade wielded by an epileptic, '. . . with every pop of my blitz I also become *you*!'

Reedy looks round at him.

'Don't look at me. Look at the wall. If the wall's not one hundred per cent the wall, it's not there! Obvious, isn't it? What else does the photographer desire but to penetrate the most intimate wiggle of the subject? What else does he require but one hundred per cent fealty! For the full fealty feeling every fibre of the subject must be captured until she fits the perfect figure of the lovely homage she declares by being who she is. Don't you feel it? Your word becoming flash? Every bounce-back of my light harmonics off you is solarising your photographer into you. No chance you can ever betray me, now! I couldn't betray myself, could I?'

Reedy says nothing. Perhaps she imparts a little extra bounce to her rear end.

'Ah, Reedy, fealty is nothing if not one hundred

per cent marriage to the moment. How pendulous you look perched on that mattress! Let me capture the tender tremolo of your fidelity in a single shutter click! Let me depict you forever at the moment of your eternally loyal surrender!'

With a deep sigh, Reedy affirms the oath.

Screwing his camera to its tripod, intensely stimulated by the scenario which he is now becoming part of, Spider explains that when the promise to perform a task is stated in a form of words enacting the promise, such as '*I do*' or '*I will*', a state is achieved of having a word do the thing it ought to do if only people would not get between the language and what it refers to. OK?

'You what?' calls Reedy, her voice muffled by the throbs of her speaking pillow.

For in the act of speaking, Spider has become intensely deflected from talking about the art of photography to being part of the photograph itself.

'What are you doing?' she asks calmly.

Stunt flying is the answer. Wing-walking. Looping the loop. Making a pluto ace anagram in his head of the word 'love', whose only possible lexical recombination is vole. He's 'going the vole' or 'chancing everything on the hope of great reward'. You don't believe me? Look it up. He's making anagrams of their names. Spider and Reedy. Reedy and Spider. As the camera, left on automatic, starts its ten second series of bulb revelations, he thinks: 'Iris pries deeds open'. How many deeds? How open the openness? How many seconds? A glimpse of their sublime entanglement in the mirror provokes: 'All I espy R. deeds'. He's getting the hang of it now. He can feel her comradely rebuttals of his brotherly thrusts. 'Depend ready, sir?' 'In deeper dryad.' 'Denser dryad pie?' 'Speedy and direr.' Sloosh, sloosh. Ripple. It's the Dark Ages all over again. Oh Daddy, let it rip, serene! No, no. Not yet. Prolongation of a baronial progress is a necessary concomitant to ensuring the devotion of the people. Airspeed. Airspeed. Airspeed.

Yesterday, Reedy bought a book of advice for girls. Following its suggestions, she employs her mind by thinking of her own country, its friendly river banks and green pastures. Its sheep. She thinks of Queen Victoria, the nineteenth century's amiable monarch, and of how in those days one's word was one's bond. She imagines the plump old queen leaning forward to pour tea for her deceased consort, and smiling regretfully as the cup brims whoopsadaisically over. What a nice sepia-coloured picture that would make! Then Spider gives a great cry. Reedy's nose is propelled forcibly into the pillow.

She clenches her eyes and thinks of the word.

THE WEB

As I approach it, all I can see is a brilliant node. Filigree lines spread outwards from it in a concentric pattern whose limits I cannot discern. Maybe stars droop like wilting blossoms from each tip of its radial network. Maybe at the outer circumference of its too–infinite–to–grasp compass, an interminably fading circle of brilliance is just fading. How should I know?

Almost immediately, I realise the object I've approached so forthrightly is not just one of many in the galaxy. It's actually the centre of the universe. It beggars any concept of size. And by the mere act of approaching it, I've become part of it.

Astro–extrilist that I am, my sense of being an inter–loper, an intruder, becomes magnified a trillion–fold. Just as well. This magnification is the power source of my nerve–driven engines. The filigree wires trill, sing and quiver as if they've detected an unusual presence and I use the extra power surge they convey to set my craft swooping far and long over the surface. Every crumb of energy I employ to stop the wires pulling me down, however, creates an even more powerful suction of contrariety. It's clear that the net is intelligent, it contains awareness. Neither for me, nor against me, it's still, in some powerful way, neither for me, nor against me. My computers cannot analyse this.

Then I realise what's happening.

At some point my nerves will no longer be able to transmit the ever-heavier burden of the one message they keep flashing to my brain, and which I persist in ignoring: *Insufficient fuel for the contemplated manoeuvre.*

I'll have no option but to set down.

AN ADDRESS AT BEDTIME

Spider holds Reedy Buttons in his arms all night long. 'Listen,' he says, holding her too tightly, 'listen!' She listens, but she can hear nothing except the rattle of his breath, the scrape of his fingernails against her flesh, the grunts of his dream.

He knows full well that she must suffer. He loves her too much to make her happy. The way she curves into him, the way he encloses her, the delicate handful of her newly ripened breasts. His breath is like the dragon-smoke of ancient insults against her nostril.

'Permanent revolution,' he says. 'It's the only way.' He waxes political, holding her in eternal quiescence, fumbling her body day and night with paralysed gestures of radical opinion. Desire is never allowed to go to sleep on Spider.

She feels the creak of his arms around her. She feels the clank of his legs, manacling her waist.

Then she hears, quite distinctly, like the ghost of seriousness haunting her ear, his cracked voice slipping through the wall of her tympanum. It's a silent tirade without content, a vanished Nuremberg rally of something inexplicably defiant, echoing through the corridors of the huge, bureaucratic headquarters of time. Is it his way of preparing, she wonders, for the day the final predictable failure is announced, and the soil you scatter gently over the dead, the soft crumbly pattering sound it makes as it falls, becomes an extinguished reminder of the spark which lingers in your eyes as you look back across the gulf of the moment in which you died?

Haven't lovers always been born, and lived, and departed, hoping things won't turn out this way?

O WHAT A LOVELY
PUNCTURE

Spider and Reedy Buttons have hired a cottage in a green valley dotted with sheep. Just over the hill is a rancorous city, but here everything is peaceful, except for the noise of the rain. It's raining cats and dogs and the thump of falling bodies drums loudly on the slate roof.

'What, my little Grimalkin, do you think of the idea that everything loses its gleam as we grow older?' He is paring his fingernails with what look like hedgecutters. 'We glorify the genitalia of our adolescence, light clings to the sexy aspirations of youth, alas by the time one is adult there is nothing left but clothes pegs and furniture . . .'

. . . a sprig of nail pings across the room . . .

'. . . but as life is all about vanishing, it's the quality of that vanishing we must concern ourselves with, wouldn't you say? It's no good trying to vanish as if we were wardrobes. We must do it with fleetness of foot . . .'

. . . a further sprig of nail hits the cat, in the eye . . .

'. . . and we shall need a lissom sense of presence, if we are going to disappear with dignity. In order to vanish one must first be here. And we must have a there to vanish in the direction of. But where are we? And what time is it? Ah, my little ear-flicker, we are like those unfortunate persons who have been left holding something an unknown person has handed us and told us not to let go of, a cable, let's say. So here we are in the middle of nowhere, gripping a hawser which disappears vertically into the clouds, at the end of which there is something with a demonstrably airborne heaviness we tug at from time to time to alleviate our boredom, and yet, and yet . . . no one returns to relieve us at our station. We cannot even see what we're holding on to. We are alone . . . Should we let the damn thing go and walk away, or remain at our post? Answerless as I am, my little whisker-waggler, all I can do is sit here and coax the creaky moorings of your body with my eyes . . .'

. . . he lays down his cutters and gazes solicitously upon Reedy Buttons' breasts, freely floating beneath the blouse of her presence . . .

'. . . ah, my dearest Reedy, what a dear, discernible shape you have! Come and sit in my lap, let me play with your tail. Listen to the rain! Before we get swept away for ever, let me cup thy breasts in the listening instruments of my palms . . .'

. . . his hand deceives her everywhere. No. His hand is deceiving itself. She too feels herself deceiving his hand. The small birds doe sing . . .

'Is it not too expensive,' asks Reedy, 'the rent we have paid for this dwelling at the top of a mud slide that may soon sweep us all away?'

'Expensive, cheap . . . what's that . . . ? Why do you babble of practicalities so? Practicalities are one-legged exhibitionists, my dearest, they will never win a race. O my little mouser, do not talk to me when I'm devoting myself to your essence. Words only get in the way . . .'

. . . as he talks they are removing each other's clothes. She sits astride him, pressing her breasts into the sockets of his eyes. He cannot see. She grips his waist with the fork of her thighs, those soft compasses of loveliness. Like a nail paring he flies up into the air with a tremendous ping . . .

'Oh!' she says. 'Oh!'

There is a Herculean rumble, a Brobdingnagian ruction. Did the earth move? Is the mud slide beginning to undulate, preparatory to carrying them away? It's neither. In the city over the hill, some urchin with a catapult has holed a vast advertising balloon which, propelled by its flatulent leak and slowly deflating as it crosses the valley, has sunk lower and lower to drape itself over their cottage, its thick, punctured elephant skin enveloping chimneys, windows and doors entirely, plunging them into a state of uttter darkness.

'Well, then,' says Spider, 'here we are! Eh? Here we are!'

DESCENDED FALCON

We take a train, the bird and I, out beyond the edges
of the city to the hills. In the empty compartment,
it perches on my glove. Alighting at an unmanned
halt, I walk out of the station, climb a stile on the
far side of the road, and then we're off, striding over
moorland. There's a view across four counties from
the ridge.

I let the bird go, watch it ride the rolling level,
steady itself and stride off, rebuffing the big wind.
You know the quotation. Brute beauty and valour
and act. Through binoculars, I follow its body-gliding
against a tower of air, sovereign over trouble. Then
a conflagration consumes me – a spreading inward
burn. How utterly I've been deceiving myself!
The falcon is plummeting downwards. I press the
field glasses so hard against my brow, the rims leave
their imprint on my skin. I'm watching the fall of a
little bag of feathers, a tiny, dying parachutist, canopy
trailing, hurtling to earth until with a small bounce it
hits the ground and lies still.

I pan the fieldglasses over the landscape. On a
small country lane, a tall woman is lowering a rifle.
She's alone. Quickly, she tosses the weapon into
the back seat of a drab-looking Volkswagen Beetle.

There's a puff of blue smoke from the exhaust as it drives off.

I pan the glasses back. A fox has the corpse in its jaws and is trotting briskly towards woodland. 'Hey!' I shout and begin to run. The fox doesn't even bother to speed up. It just keeps going, the feathered thing in its mouth. There's a tantivy, and over a hill come huntsmen and hounds. Another pack, followed by two red-jacketed yahoos on horseback ride up the hill in a pincer movement. Since when does the foxhunt not just go hell for leather in a straight line? The fox stops dead, not knowing which way to go. Two packs of beagles fall upon it. Spurts of scarlet increase their frenzy. The fox's detached head is held up. There are cheers. Someone waves the fox's brush.

I focus the glasses on them. An older man rides up to a younger and jovially daubs the young man's cheeks with the fox's heart. A flask is going round and liquid is being gulped down. Foxblood seems to rise in my craw. The ruddy faces of the riders have become wildly elasticated. It's as if the fingers of a drunken puppet master were thrust up through their necks, distending jaws and eyes in apocalyptic glee. The distant chorus of a song of wassail mounts to my brain and I feel like a fatally involved spectator at the falling-down games. How could I have allowed myself to witness this hole opening in the afternoon? As punishment for my own stupidity, I force myself to lift the glasses beyond the circle of huntsmen, and steadily follow one remaining feather wafting on a current of air towards the trees.

SADNESS INC.

Spider has been appointed chairman of Global Sadness Incorporated. In Tower Doleful, he gives the sadness team an anti-pep talk, inspiring them with mumpish discordancy.

'Gentlemen! What is it we seek? Sadness! The true sadness, the imperishable, unlovely sadness of eternity!'

The faces of ten lachrymose underlings illuminate with dolour.

'What do we have instead, gentlemen? Happy endings, gentlemen, with glycerine teardrops on their film-starry cheeks! And what do those teardrops represent? Vainglorious sadness, gentlemen! Where is the face of the real sadness, her eyes like windows spattered with icy rain, her mouth hanging off its hinges like a well-kicked door?'

Ten be-suited hirelings gleam lugubriously at him.

'My friends! What causes these vaingloriously sad-happy endings? Hope, gentlemen! But O my goodness, how inauthentic this hope is! Does not real sadness, gentlemen, lie in the admission that hope is well and truly deceased? '

The listeners emit a long groan of post-cognitive cognition.

'Gentlemen, we must annihilate once and for all the very form, texture and substance of hope! For this hope builds dominions. It builds minuscule colonies in sanguine little hearts. And from such tiny settlements, as we know, great Babylons of Happy Awfulness are apt to arise.'

Ten shiny and somehow hopeful faces attempt to eradicate from their expressions any sign of misplaced expectation.

'What is the nature of this sadness of which I speak?' Spider's teeth crack like mordant nuts. 'Is it the sadness that admits brotherhood? No, gentlemen, it rejects the concept of fraternity even as it shakes your hand. Is it the sadness that seeks out equality? Gentlemen, what sadness knows is that there is always a boot stamping on the fingers which grip the rung below it. And when it hears the word "liberty", gentlemen, what does sadness do? It rattles a ring of gaolers' keys. Shout the word "revolution!", it calls up a tumbril. Say "filth", "touch", "hunger", you will be as close to sadness as it is possible, far away, to get, but how far away is that? There is no reciprocity in sadness; it will never cleanse you, stroke you, feed you. Sadness will never take you in its arms, gentlemen, for its essence is solitude and how can solitude experience the feeling of an embrace? What, in fact, *is* an embrace? Is it not simply another person, bringing you inauthentic hope?'

A penetrating ululation keens upward and outward. It occupies the air-conditioning ducts, floats in the lift-shafts, consumes the building in mouthfuls of audio–tactile distress. Tower Doleful is a psycho-spiritual skyrise of brute desolation, a materialist wail shivering through the testes of the universe.

'Hearkeners to the mournful word, listen to my lyric note of unstrung cheerlessness! How shall we raise sadness to its true elevation, and set the dejected Statue of Misery once again in its rightful place? How shall we communicate the true spirit of grief to every man's mind?'

A hanging-dog of a doldrum-inspissated person, no less than the Chief Superintendent of Woe and Griping Gloom, hauls himself sunkenly to his feet and croaks: 'The picture, Spider. Give us the picture!'

'Aye!' they call. It is like a wind. It is a plea. A yearning distress note of no fixed address.

With a deathly smile, Spider crumples in a resolute fist the small working model of martyrdom the office staff have laboured for months to construct from ordinary matchsticks.

'Today's picture,' he says, 'is that of the truly meritless man, whose past does not bear thinking about.'

'*Aye . . . eee!*'

'He emerges from a subway under the river, into a choking November afternoon of rain and purchases.'

'*Aye . . . eee!*'

'He wears a raincoat and a beret. He is on his way home from Felicity, his lover, who lives at the opposite end of the metropolis. And whatever transpired in her dwelling we shall pass over in silence. Whether he travels north or south, what mode of conveyance he uses, what memories he replays in his head, what cries, what little screams he may remember hearing, these are of no particular significance to him, they are merely primitive exercises in destiny, for he knows his future is contained in the building he has been sent to, and he knows the overwhelming sense of despondency and mortification which will afflict him when he enters it.'

'Aye . . . eee!'

'What is this building? Is it a court of law? A university? An aliens registry office? No, gentlemen! It's a supermarket!'

'Aye . . . eee!'

'He shuffles along its aisles. He picks up merchandise and puts it down again. But Felicity's errand has to be carried out, for love, as we know, must be paid for. He reads labels, compares prices. Could anything be more futile? Ah, gentlemen, the price of passion comes steep, or not at all, does it not? Regard his posture. Does it not suggest a communicant in the Church of Excluded Hope? Watch him place items in the covert pockets of his raincoat. Outside the drizzle is drizzling, in Apocalypse Villas, in Bottomless Crescent, in Crack O' Doom Close, along Agony Boulevard, down Spifflication Way. Of course he doesn't want to be there; that's the reason he's there. His absent presence, gentlemen, is a candle lit against the delusion of hope . . .'

'Aye . . . eee!'

'And what he knows, he knows, gentlemen. It's a knowledge which is borne right through him on a wave of rain-smell as he steps from the shop with the articles he has stolen in his pockets . . .'

'Aye . . . eee!'

'What does he know, gentlemen? He has fore-knowledge of his own arrest, of course!'

'Aye . . . eee!'

'And who will apprehend him? Naturally, the police!'

'Aye . . . eee!'

'What words will they use? Ah, it is a sad construct they will construct. A rigmarole of risible rectitude, gentlemen, nothing more and nothing less!'

'Aye . . . eee!'

'And a cool wind is blowing rain across the park. Cars splash as they pass. What has the culprit placed in his pockets? Biscuits, gentlemen! Could anything be sadder than biscuits? There's your picture! Has he not truly earned the words of reproach that babble in his face? And Felicity's smell still lingers on his fingertips. With what deep and ineffable melancholy will he now endure the remarkable descending use-lessness of the future in whose direction he will be frogmarched . . . ?'

'Aye . . . eee!'

'That, gentlemen, is sadness!'

VERA VENTURA

Those of us who have kept the planet going for so long, toiling in our overalls for a few blubs a week, know of course who they are. Beneath the great Plexiglas canopy which repels the foetid atmosphere of earth, we scurry to produce and consume, and watch from afar as they meet on the high gantries to which no visible ladders or staircases lead. They wear dark clothes and shake hands incessantly. We see them rise from the canopy into the outer atmosphere in small craft with whirling rotors and wonder where they are headed.

My companion in the bunk above mine is an old man. He murmurs of catastrophes in his sleep. Occasionally, when we are alone, he looks at me and says:

'You think Spider holds the key to the truth?'

It is of course forbidden to respond to any question with a 'no', a negation being the most intolerable form of insubordination. I have an attack of coughing.

'Would you like to be free?'

The words 'free' and 'freedom' are proscribed words. One has only a very dim idea of what they mean. Anyone using them is quite likely to disappear.

'The word you employ refers to a state with which I am unfamiliar.'

But with that reply, I have sailed too close to the airducts. We are arrested and taken God knows where. I am shown into a room. Spider sits behind a huge desk. I would know those features anywhere. They wear a look that is puzzled, quizzical, humorous, tired and full of patient apprehension.

'You hesitated,' he remarks. 'All we ask of our citizens is an automatic response, the perfect semblance of conviction. Yet you had the arrogance to hesitate. You *considered* the question.'

I look into his dark, impassioned eyes. I think of the old man. His treachery doesn't matter to me now. They will have sent him cabin-solo to the asteroids. What does Spider have in mind for me?

The door slithers open and Vera Ventura stands there, a fibrillating spak-gun in her gloved right hand. She wears a brilliant silver spacesuit and her brown hair is coiled in a fetching bun. Up till now she has only been a legend. Someone who haunts the cosmic wainscot. Yet here she is, advancing into the room, giving me a smile and directing a look of interplanetary contempt at Spider, who has thrown up his hands in surrender. Vera Ventura grips me by the elbow and we back out of the door. As we turn to run, I suddenly realise we have entered another room. A very similar room. Spider sits behind a huge desk. He wears a look that is puzzled, quizzical, humorous, tired and full of patient apprehension.

Vera Ventura grips me by the elbow and we back

out of the door. As we turn to run, I suddenly realise we have entered another room. Spider sits behind a huge desk. He wears a look that is puzzled, quizzical, humorous, tired and full of patient apprehension.

Vera Ventura grips me by the elbow . . .

MURDER

It's a simple matter to terminate her life, but I terminate mine first to ensure no one will lay the blame at my door. I hang myself in the hall, but the corpse doesn't please me, lolling there with its neck awry and the tongue hanging out, thick and extruded, like a piece of German sausage. I take hundreds of pills and wait for the rush of extinction to engulf me. The man comes to repair the dishwasher. Soon he has all the little bits and pieces laid out on the tiles. I feel terrible. Obviously the dishwasher will never work again. I go upstairs, take out my father's old service revolver and blow my brains out. They slither down the mirror like a failed omelette and I gaze at myself between the gobbets: surely I look dead enough now? I go downstairs again and stand ostentatiously in the kitchen, but the repairman doesn't look up. That's all the confirmation I need. I am obviously truly dead – now I can go out and commit murder with impunity.

I call her up and tell her I'm leaving her. She wants to know who I'm leaving her for. Someone I've never met, I say. Someone anonymous with whom I have a blind contract of union till death. Long silence on the line. Can we meet just once more? For old time's sake? We arrange a rendezvous on a slash of green in the middle of the city, a tiny oasis of nature between buses and taxis.

When I arrive, she's already waiting. My long-dead heart is beating like a time bomb. Her beauty assails me from the other side of the street; her tall, willowy figure, the long brown hair, the loose silky clothes she wears, the impertinent cheerfulness with which she tries to humour me. How can I explain to her my moral being has told me I must stop clinging to life and prepare myself for resurrection as a fly? I'm carrying an arsenal in my bag: Domestic hammer. Cheese wire. Electric tack gun. Plastic bag. Waiter's corkscrew.

Underneath the statue of Old Bill in the middle of the green triangle is a park bench. We sit on it and she embraces me. Her cheek is wet with tears. 'Why?' she asks. One has sought out the condition of death precisely in order not to have to answer this question. I stab her. Then I place the plastic bag over her head. I sink back under the shadow of Old Bill's bronze waistcoat, load my tack gun and close my eyes. When I open them, Spider is sitting next to her, timing the snorts and gasps of her final moments with a pocket watch.

'You seem to have achieved the desired effect,' he murmurs. 'It's taking a while, though.'

'Don't talk to me, I'm dead,' I reply. To emphasise the nature of my condition I cut my own throat.

'Aha,' says Spider.

Then, using my tack gun, I staple myself to the bench, right through the heart.

'Move along, please. You're causing a disturbance,' he says.

I wrench myself free and slouch away. As I do so, I hear him engage her in measured conversation: 'Have you known him long, my dear? Where did you meet him? What was his opening line? Mmm. And when did you first notice he had begun to change . . . ?'

SPIDER RIDES OUT

Carrying a lantern, my host leads me down to the cellar, opening a trap door to the black river beneath, ladling the chill cleanness from a stoup into our glasses. We drink and drink, talking of water and the origin of thirst.

Then we climb the wooden stairway to the room with the ancient fireplace. A table is set for dinner. As we eat, I think of the fields sloping away from the house, and of the woman waiting for me upstairs, passing naked in front of the window, her silhouette visible in the thrown light of a candle flame. I imagine myself already with her, our bedroom conversation, its illumined gaiety making the shadows of two heads dance upon the ceiling. I imagine the single man in his cloak, waiting on the cobbles below for the horse to be brought out that will take him far. I imagine him looking up, dipping into his tobacco pouch and frowning to himself as we extinguish the candle for bed.

'By Our Lady!' says Spider. 'By the Toenails of Christ!'

When the time really comes for me to retire, I climb the stair, thinking of him riding away with a clatter, bending to push at gates that swing easily open to his stick and swing as easily shut, no need of dismounting, the known path taking him up the hill towards the sky, the trees along the rim.

Stopped upon a half-landing, I light a troubling patch of darkness with the taper in my hand. The rider, too, up there on the rim, reins in his horse.

I hear her low voice out of the shadows. 'Yes,' I reply, 'it's me.' And as I bend toward her opened embrace, where she lies bare-shouldered on the pillow, fierce arms reach up for the rider, pulling him from the horse. A foreign phrase rips his ear, blood fills his mouth.

'God's Potatoes!' cries Spider, staggering and feeling his injuries. Her tongue enters me, almost like a knife. Awkwardly, Spider has drawn his weapon. The moon's clarity shows an emptiness in the clearing where the sweep and hiss of a blade keep his assailants at bay. 'Eight times through the doublet, four through the hose, sword hacked like a handsaw!' cries Spider. And her body is hot against mine, cleaving hard to my frame, almost the length of a sword.

As his shout echoes through my brain, I remember with exact clarity the taste of water in my mouth, its coolness, its freshness. I feel its invisible movement deep below in the river underneath the earth.

PIRATICAL SPIDER

Long Johns Brass, Gold and Silver, Captains Bluebeard, Bligh and Spider have all assembled upon a desert-island beach. The surf licks at their scuffed boots like a blind beggar snuffling the pockmarked skin of a naked prostitute. Behind the villainous conference which is taking place on the otherwise printless sand rises the volcano.

It's as if they've sailed through a million years of storybooks and emerged like this, none the worse for wear, grown up and stinking. When children weren't looking, they slit the throat of the kindly old merchant for his maps and took his daughters by force one after the other behind a huge barrel marked *Gunpowder*. When the children stirred and opened their eyes sleepily, the pirates came out from behind the barrel doing up their breeches and waving cheerfully. At confession time, they intrigued Father Godd with semi-literate barings of preposterous breasts. Their professions of love and courage were so outrageously fraudulent, Godd was impressed. Indeed, he put on cutlass, cummerbund and cocked hat, and joined them.

Taking their swords, they begin to slice the foliage of the island to pieces. With makeshift barges hacked from noble, thousand-year-old trees, they ford the unbridgeable rivers that lead towards its heart. Naturally as they get closer to the treasure, they murder one another. Captain Spider hits Father Godd over the head with a wellington boot and is left in sole possession of the map.

He climbs down into the volcano, his blade-like eyes sharp from the whetstone of struggle, his blackguard fingers driving like spikes into the sides of the rock.

Then, from underneath, he hears a thunderous belch. Sensing that something is about to blow, Spider goes into life-saving reverse. The children sit up in bed, watching a dressing-gown shift on the bedroom door. It seems to them that the garment is quite possibly alive, trying to get away from something terrible and incomprehensible.

Spider has his eye on the little gleam of light at the top of the volcano. To hell with the treasure. He drops the map. 'Pull your pillows over your head!' he roars. 'This is no time to expect the end of the story!'

But the children are staring into the darkness, their dilated pupils gleaming like the eyes of rats.

'We'll continue the story tomorrow!' shouts Spider.

What would the children like to happen? For an ironical angel to pluck him by the collar from the fire? For him to be frazzled retributively to a crisp? A spew of incandescent lava comes barrelling up the cone of the volcano towards Spider's boots. The children press their little hands together and exchange glances. Then a door opens in the side of the volcano, a pale white arm reaches out and draws him in. The door closes and everything is cool. There's the sound of water running along rock, the swish of ferns. The belching of the earth fades. Spider opens his eyes and sees naked boys and girls swimming in a deep black pool.

She smiles down at him, his beautiful, calm saviour. She's what every island protects, what the mob is always subdued by, what no footprints across the sand have ever led to, and here she lies, next to him, smiling . . .

The children snuggle down again and close their eyes, which is just as well.

Spider has spotted the map jutting from her apron pocket.

IN THE CELLAR OF
DWARFSLOPER TOWERS

A flash of lightning illuminates the weathered sign-board which reads: *Home for the Incurably Deluded (Dr J. Spider Rembrandt, res. physician).* There is a growl of thunder, a screech of wind and the rain begins to fall. High in the turrets of Dwarfsloper Towers a single light is burning. In the darkness of the well-carpeted and empty cellar, a tape recorder clicks on, triggered by an electrical fault. Dr Rembrandt's nasal tones announce to dark rows of unoccupied seats: *Case History One: A Fish*, and a gruff, slightly distant voice begins hesitantly to speak:

'It's a long time ago now, a sunny weekday afternoon. I'm strolling in the park as far as the ornamental lake, with its ironwork bridge at one end. You know the one. A great pike face rears up out of the smooth black water and comes at me, its prehistoric fish jaws cleaving the surface, water pouring off its great head, and, well, anyone'd do the same, doctor, I step back from the edge. There are children playing, mothers gossiping, a blackbird whistling and I'm the only person witnessing this. The mighty muscle of an aged fish heart is driving the creature straight at me and I think: O God! The life of this fish thing was a blank reckoning, deep in the mud and now its jaws have opened on nothing and here I am looking down its throat into an abyss, doctor. It comes thrashing its thick body through the water towards me and I just stand there . . . paralysed . . . staring . . . and then it vanishes. It simply vanishes, doctor. I've so often wanted to tell people about it. Make this report . . . for years . . . and years . . . and years . . .'

The tape continues to hiss. The green light on the machine glows. It's as if the empty chairs are waiting expectantly for what will follow. The ancient spools revolve slowly. Dr Rembrandt clears his throat and says tinnily: *Case History Two: Chinamen.* A light tenor voice with the hint of an Australian accent speaks without pauses, hesitations or even sniffs:

'Chinamen know how to do it. You know those little vans they have on street corners, playing the gong version of 'Greensleeves', like ice-cream salesmen? No, of course you don't. I'm the only person who knows about them. But you could guess why they're there, couldn't you doc? They're there to rewind us, so we can play our lives' tune differently. Memories are . . . well . . . they're just too much, eh doc? We were never apart in those days, but she left me. Went to Norway. Of all places. Norway. With somebody else. Last week, doc, I went out and bought a job lot of last year's calendars. Fjords, salmon fishermen, wooden houses . . . Norway. Then I went home, took a screwdriver and defaced them. I annihilated Norway. What I thought was this, doc: I'd get memory to put things back they were, make them alright again. I mean, if you could put memory in charge, what would it say, doc? It would say: go back and do it again properly. Then it would all be the way you wanted to have it in the first place, wouldn't it? So, of course, I went out looking for the Chinamen. I could hear them playing 'Greensleeves' in the next street, but when I went round the corner there was no one there. Like telephone boxes, eh doc? Never there when you want one! Doc, that's why I need your help. If I can get you to see them, we'll all be able to see them. We'll all be able to rewind our lives and start again, properly. I mean I know it's going to make people like you, doc, well . . . unnecessary . . . but we need those Chinamen with that ideogram technology of theirs and their little vans on every street, with smoke-stacks protruding, giving off blue puffs of promising smoke and little blokes sticking their heads out and grinning, and we'll all be queuing up to be admitted one by one . . .'

The tape player continues to run, the big fourteen-inch spool has a long way to go yet. Beyond the cellar window there are three vivid flashes followed by the rumbling dynamite of thunder. In a fuse box on the wall something fizzes and begins to smoke. From the tape machine's speakers, a background series of fearsome squeaks, howls and inarticulate cries grows steadily in volume, melding into an intolerable jabber to which the empty chairs seem deeply attentive as flames reach the curtains and the building starts to burn.

UNDER SURVEILLANCE

'Bring up camera four,' says Spider.

In hat and cigarette, a man hurries past ripped hoardings, splashes through puddles of water, wades through piles of garbage left over from the last municipal workers' strike . . .

'Camera ten,' says Spider.

She, in the terror of need, walks across a rain-soaked garden, the wet boughs brush her forehead. Her coat is open, her handbag carelessly undone. The gate squeaks open and she knots the scarf she has hastily thrown around her neck . . .

Spider sits in his flickering office at the criminal-investigations department, filing his nails. 'Scarves of contrition we are used by all, worn by all,' he observes to nobody and apropos of nothing.

From different ends of the city, prosodic squalls of wind and evening light tap like knuckles at the window of the heart. Tap tap tap. They want to be let in.

'What is a knock at the window, Bastet, but the physical manifestation of a sob?' remarks Spider.

Bastet gives a start, blinks, miaows, yawns, wraps his tail the other way and goes back to sleep.

The door opens. The lovers embrace each other.

They are on the bed. They are naked. The monitor screen fizzes and goes blank.

'Yeah, yeah,' says Spider. 'What begins well, ends badly. Bring up camera twelve.' More unfathomable fizzing. Then he hears a phrase, spoken in an undertone. A woman's voice says, quite clearly: 'Soul-burglars.'

'Soul-burglars, eh?' says Spider, scribbling. 'With or without a hyphen?'

A shooting star crosses the monitor screen. He stares. It's in the shape of a woman, falling – a single streak of light across a vesper sky.

'Vesper sky,' he mutters. 'How did I come to write that?' He scores it out and writes, 'severe interference'.

Someone is calling out, a voice in suffering . . . the despairing cry of a lover to the beloved . . .

Spider looks at his shorthand: 'I hope the secretaries don't read this. They'll burst into tears and take the day off.' He takes out a flag-sized handkerchief and blows his nose, trumpet-like. Bastet looks up. 'At least you –' says Spider, gazing into the cat's grey eyes '– even down on the floor like that – at least you have some sense of dignity.'

He reaches for a knob and tunes to the weather forecast.

A MYTHICAL BEAST

I'm going up the stairs behind a woman. My eyes follow the neat bones of her ankles on the risers above me. Spider brushes past on the way down. He appraises the woman on the staircase and then looks me straight in the eye, his face wearing a detestable smirk. Whether deliberately or by accident, he nudges my shoulder as he passes.

On the first landing a woman leans against an open door. Her dressing-gown is sluttishly ajar over bra and panties. She regards us without curiosity as we pass.

Outside the apartment on the next landing, a naked black woman, with close-cropped hair and protuberant nipples, is silently haranguing a pale white youth who cowers back against the wall in his underpants. No sound emerges from her contorted mouth. His whimpers are just a suggestion in my mind. All I hear as we go by their dumb show is the clack of my companion's high heels on the stair, and street sounds coming through the open door at the bottom of the stairwell.

On the next landing, terrible groans emanate from the interior of an apartment. The woman I'm following enters. In the bedroom, a middle-aged man is crouched in the dog position on the bed, receiving the attentions of a slender man with an all-over sun-parlour tan, an earring, and what looks like a knuckleduster on his right fist. The suntanned man wears a mask. As he drives forward contemptuously from the hips, the middle-aged man cries out. As well he might.

My companion goes up to the suntanned man and chides him with two swift slaps of a fan across his cheek. Then she turns, beckons me to follow, and we climb to the top of the stairs.

She unlocks the door of the apartment and draws me inside. I haven't yet managed to see her face properly. She was standing away from the streetlamp and it was the low phrases of her solicitation that immediately arrested me. They were so unusual. What she had asked me was a question no woman had ever asked me before. I'm waiting for her to find the light switch. It's dark. I hear a rustle and feel her breath, her hands. She ties a blindfold round my eyes.

The clicking sound of a switch. Inside the dark bandage round my eyes, I can see only tiny silver pinpoints of light. I raise my arms obediently so she can remove my clothes. She pulls me close and I realise she has removed hers too. My fingers settle like butterflies at her throat. With my right hand, I trace the contours of her face, trying to visualise her. Then my hand slides downwards to her thighs, into the join of her V, and I feel with astonishment how she's streaming there with womanly desire.

We fall athwart the bed. Her legs cross over

my back and her ankles lock there. I feel like the blindfolded bull led trustingly away, exhibiting that customary innocent bravery characteristic of a mythical beast, plodding down a pitch-dark forest path, so patient and yet ignorant of its fate. Through the trees a spark will flicker in a tiny cottage window, an ancient rusty oil lamp will flare and a room in a magical clearing at the end of a mysterious journey will light up. That's how they tell it. The lamp will illuminate not just the room of a small cottage, not just the room I'm in, but all the rooms of my life, a dowdy series of them, each one with a bed, a melancholy beast, an overturned chair, and a desert stretching to the horizon.

The strange bellow I let loose at this point is magnified into something unearthly that surprises even me. She joins the cacophonic wail of her release to mine. Then we roll apart. I lie exhausted, staring into the folds which bind me, close my eyes and fall asleep.

Later, the mythical beast wakes up, alone, on a grassy bank, by a stream. He removes his blindfold and stares around. His clothes are on a verdant knoll under a tree, in an untidy heap. He puts them on. His shoes and socks, however, are missing. A summer wind stirs the leaves and there is a scent of pines in the heat. Nothing else moves. He is completely alone. Feeling in his pocket for money and credit cards, he reassures himself that everything's there. No deal was struck. He is perplexed. Mythical beasts are dumb, foolish, incontinent creatures.

He closes his eyes again and gropes his way forward, hoping his sightlessness will retrieve the situation. He feels a door, and then, under bare feet, cool tiles. The bathroom. He opens his eyes, but the door has swung shut and it's pitch black in there. He reaches out to the switch and puts on the light.

In lipstick, scrawled across the mirror, are the words *I love you.*

RESPIRATION

'Her breath will blow life into you,' murmurs Spider.
'Here in the shade of tobacco trees, at the end of small
gardens, beneath rainy beeches . . . This sweet, sober
air . . . It is like a kind of music becoming distinct
which we have not listened to carefully enough,
or words we have wrongly understood suddenly
righting themselves . . .'

I take out my pistol.

'Let her presence be your anima,' says Spider.
'Take the wafer of herself on your tongue, and let
it dissolve.'

I spin the chamber.

'Breathe. That is the only thing you have left.
Inhale the tender contents of her into your lungs
and feel the pounding of your temples abate, feel
the inward-inching, down-drawing focusing of your
blood, the perfect slow-steady-slow of your heart . . .'

I put a bullet into Spider's skull. His face deflates
and then puffs up again like a spring-back rubber
mould.

'Breathe. She is not far away. It's years since she
thought of you. But every breath of oxygen you
absorb restores her to herself.'

I put the rest of the bullets into the earnest

sermon-like fuselage of his demeanour. But Spider is like the unkillable thing in one of those horror films. He appears to die and then comes back to life, each time more subtly mutilated, each time in some grotesque way more insinuatingly alive.

'Breathe,' he says. All that is left of his face is his nose, against which the upper lip flaps like a crow's wing. I watch in fascinated repulsion.

'As you breathe, you will feel how she is breathing, in Norway, on a fishing smack sailing up a fjord somewhere. As *she* breathes, she will feel how the soles of your feet are glued to the pavement of this dirty city. She will hear the fragments of conversation at your ear, she will sense how you are buffeted this way and that by passers-by, laughing and shouting, while you stand cursing your own hesitation, locked in the trap of not being able to choose from all the possible routes you could take from here.

'Breathe . . .'

WIFE TO THE KING OF EGYPT

My father, the Pharaoh, is ageing, infertile and use-less. His sacrifice is planned for Tuesday, but until the moment the Grand Vizier plunges in the dagger, the old man's word is law. He rails at me that I spend too much time tickling the Asiatic dwarf dancer, not seeking a wife. From Memphis, Edfu and Thebes, he summons the Nomarchs' daughters – but they're too thin, too fat, their noses too small, their teeth irregular, their ears too big.

As we climb the steps to the throne room, the Pharoah, my father, absent-mindedly fondles the bot-tom of a peasant woman who is scrubbing the stairs. I catch a whiff of her and make a wide detour.

Seated on his throne, with the Grand Vizier in attendance, the King, my father, permits himself a lugubrious smile. In the lower palace, he says, is an energetic serving woman, who would make an excellent wife. Then he turns to the Grand Vizier, and decrees I shall marry her.

I refuse passionately, but the King, my father, is expressionless. His scarab ring catches the light. Out of the window, I can see Omentutnoh, the architect appointed to build my pyramid, scrambling over blocks of hewn stone. My father, the Pharaoh, points out he can take whoever he likes into his own tomb, and if he takes Omentutnoh, I'll be short of an architect. No tomb for my corpse, no colloquy with Osiris. Without conversation, eternity will seem very long.

The silence which follows this feels almost as long. If there's one thing I know, it's that you need a solid tomb to spend eternity in chatting to Osiris, and Omentutnoh is the man to build it.

But marriage to a stinking peasant . . .

The Grand Vizier, Amenspiderotep, a man I sometimes regard as mother, directs an eyebrows-raised regard at my father, the King, the Pharoah, who returns it deadpan. Whatever I do, it won't be the right decision. I hedge my bets, accept my father's edict with good grace, and go for well-built accommodation in the afterlife.

Naturally I won't be allowed to meet my betrothed before Tuesday. I make it forcefully plain to Amenspiderotep that the woman will have to be cleaned up and given raiment befitting a queen. The Grand Vizier performs a bow so low the tip of his nose brushes the mosaics. Then he exits backwards, bowing all the way. Why couldn't I have had a real mother, with breasts, and cradling arms?

In the ritual period which follows, I try to make peace with my father. Ignoring me, he reclines upon the couch, trying to gather strength for the day of his exodus. I confront him with the unreasonableness of his actions. He doesn't appear to be listening. I read the inscription worked round the profile of a hook-nosed woman on the small stone tablet beside his couch. It reads: *Come eventide the sky shall swallow up the sun; come dawn the sky shall bear its fiery child again.* I'd like to ask my father who the woman is. I reach for his hand, but from under half-closed lids he detects this gesture of filial questioning, half-solicitation, and pulls his hand beneath his cloak.

Tuesday arrives, as Tuesdays will. I ride to Heliopolis, flanked by twenty-four horsemen. They've already brought my father, the Pharaoh, on a litter, and next to him, in the temple, stands my bride. She's wearing a mask and an ankle-length cloak of gold braid. Outside, the whole population, it seems, is dancing a frenzied prayer-dance. The Vizier consecrates our union. The blood of a goat is dripped on our linked hands. Then we devour the spoils of a hippopotamus hunt.

As we eat, the crowd roars in uninterrupted jubilation.

Afterwards we lead the Pharoah, my father, to The Great Slab. The sacrificial victim, who has imbibed more wine than it behoves an adventurer facing the ultimate ordeal, is made to recline upon it. Two of his favourite wives are present, their faces pale. They know, of course, that afterwards they will be summarily strangled by the Nubian slave Dampferfaht. Several Nomarchs are in attendance. There's a scribe or two, the Grand Vizier, myself and bride. As a shaft of sunlight enters the temple, we commence the neck jive of farewell. Amenspiderotep holds the sword in a flame, withdraws the glowing blade, grasps my own hand so that both of us grip the weapon, and we plunge it deep into the victim's chest. I'm obliged to lend my considerable strength to Amenspiderotep's enfeebled thrust. He gives me a sly nod of encouragement. My father, the ex-King, shivers like a dog throwing off water, and departs with a rattle for his eternal colloquy with Osiris. Behind me, I hear two sharp cracks, followed by thuds. Now the Grand Vizier and all the priests proclaim me Ra Ra the Second. The mask of Horus, the falcon, is placed over my head. My bride and I are led deeper and deeper into the temple. In an inner chamber, upon a dais surrounded by four wide, shallow steps, is the Pharaonic couch.

Amenspiderotep lifts the mask from my bride and removes her cloak. She's a mature, handsome woman, at least ten years older than me. The skin of her face is weathered, darker than the fresh chestnut of her body. She stands in her bare feet, wearing nothing except green eye paint, anklet rings and a beaded necklace of jasper and onyx. I stare at the bushes of hair beneath her armpits, the densely-coiled jet triangle at her groin, the lines on her belly of one who has borne children. Her face is impassive. She has the powerful arms of a working woman. I feel intensely exhilarated. The Grand Vizier assists her onto the couch and she lies back. Bastet the cat springs from nowhere and sprawls between the gnawed studs of her teats. There's a murmur from the watchers.

The Grand Vizier intones: 'O Geb, your arms

are around her, the Osiris, the lady of the house Henut-wedjebu. You have brightened her face and opened her eyes.'

That's true. At moments like this all eyes are on the woman. I remove my cloak and there are more murmurs. I shoo away the cat, and arrange myself between the opened legs of my bride. Through the eyeholes of the mask, I regard her expressionless face. I note the delicate, erotic curve of her hooked nose and, as I enter her, provoking excited cries from the priests, and a whoop from the Grand Vizier, I realise who exactly she is. The inhuman oath I unleash at that moment swirls and wisps smokily in the rafters above the couch as if to presage an endless procreative dawn of fiery children.

MORE PINGS FROM THE SPRINGS

Here on the seventh floor of Alarum Heights there is a noise of hammering and drills. In the lobby, I know, workmen are installing themselves. They will rebuild the villa as a medieval fortress. These days it is a frequently expressed wish of customers to have a moat and a drawbridge. When I make my occasional forays out for groceries, I often trip over cables and equipment. When I return, I notice the perimeter wall has grown another three feet. By evening the sounds of building work diminish and I am left to concentrate on myself. I stare at my reddened eyes in the mirror. Have I been weeping?

Well, and if I have been weeping, so what? Might they not have been tears of laughter? How does one tell the difference? Why, if at all, was I ever accommodated here? Why did I move? Don't I have a family, a home? Have I lost my memory. My money? I cannot recall if I ever had a memory, so there is no answering that one. I distinctly remember some people with whom I often had cause to expostulate – so perhaps I did have a family. And if I can remember that, maybe I had some money. But why does the bed creak so? I have never used such a loquacious instrument. If only I could understand what those plangencies might signify.

I imagine an earthquake splitting the whole house open like a peach to reveal a stone in the centre, myself. Evening has drawn in and without light there is nothing to stop the submarines coming up the plughole. I stagger back to the bed and fling myself down upon a heap of what I conjecture to be nothing more than a decade of vile gossip. I can sense periscopes swivelling in my direction. I ignore them. The window blank gleams with the reflected light of the city. I get up, lean out and look over that dull tract of nothing. Slowly, I let down my hair.

Spider grabs it as if I were Rapunzel or something. I can feel the weight of him pulling the scalp off the top of my skull.

Effortfully but surely he comes up. I can smell his breath on my face: doombreath. He grins at me, that bewildering, shelterless grimace of mutually ironic camaraderie that sends shivers down into my trolleybus star platform shoes. Then he hauls himself into the room, casts around for somewhere to sit, and plops his weight on the bed.

Not so long ago someone else had been there, crying out something I mistook for a declaration of love. He lifts his eyes to mine.

I stare into his pupils. I know I'm looking at the Robin Hood of déjà vu. I know he robs the poor and gives to the rich. I've heard his clients crying from their silken beds of distress: 'More! More!'

'Well?' he asks.

I pace up and down. The feelings I'm having resemble a strange encounter between a girl I once loved and the exam results of my youth.

Gently, as if I'm going mad, I ask him what he's come for.

'The murder weapon,' he says.

He places the flat of his hands beside him and presses up and down, producing a few demonstrative *grunks*. I gaze at the narrow, domestic immobility of it, shoved up hard against the wall.

'Take it,' I murmur. 'It will tell you all you want to know.'

He does.

JAPAN

Spider is walking along Milton Road. The rain is like Japan, crowded yet orderly, and queues of cars shudder forwards on shouts and smoke. With a yammer, the helicopter goes over, filming the motorists' predicament. Spider teases himself with the jaw-kicks, leg-hammers and elbow-stonks of Japanese philosophy. He is head-delicate and the rain makes origami boots of his thought.

To escape the exhaust fumes, Spider turns into a park, goes past a green pavilion, rusting grass rollers, a disused cricket scoreboard. He walks the gauntlet of a line of dripping acacias and continues along a muddy track lined with old Sunday newspapers. Across wooden fences, he can see manicured gardens in which the vegetation seems to have suffocated in the upright position. He peers over to see if he can detect life there. Nothing appears to be moving. No screams. No shadows.

He goes over a small bridge. Below it, a stream pockmarked with rain is drawing one last breath for an asthmatic city. Fallen willows lie across it, their branches rising and falling in the current, much like a girl who has slit her wrists in the bath. Finally, he turns into Shelley Drive, an ordinary suburban

street. As far as the eye can see, Ford Britannias line the kerb, parked nose to tail, like museum pieces. Surely this must indicate the citizens are in? Spider walks along the housefronts, each similar porch, each similar gable. In one of these houses lived the woman in question. He has an image of her, proffering a bowl of rice soup in both hands, bowing respectfully as you'd expect. The houses seem so vacant, it's difficult to tell which of them it might be. Have the occupants entirely dissolved into their own soup? Shelley Drive leads into Tennyson Avenue, which brings him back to Eliot Boulevard, a stinking and infernal queue of rusting, smoking vehicles.

On the car radios the disc jockeys are playing banzai music — music for the end of the suicidal calm. The cars inch onward into the sound of the disc jockey's jabber. It's as if everyone is waiting to die — the faint reverb of Hiroshima before a memory attack. Overhead, planes are rolling in, their undercarriages drooping like haemorrhoids. As they pass low in the sky, on a collision course with the horizon, they leave a kind of scream hanging in the air, like an animal that has been hunted out of its habitat for ever. Spider looks up cautiously. He desires the solitude of not being here, the solitude of a place where cherry blossom dispels nightmares and rainy breezes waft a sweet smell into the nostrils, where silence is heavenly — not like Japan.

It's impossible to cross the road on Eliot Boulevard. The cars leave no spaces for pedestrians to squeeze through to the other side. Spider waits patiently.

Hours pass. Finally, he pulls up his hood, like a brigand monk, steps off the pavement and, flashing an imaginary samurai sword, arrests the forward creep of vehicles and prostrates himself in the road, the length of his spine measuring the white line down the middle, his legs and arms stretched out like a starfish. The traffic halts. Patience begins to simmer. It boils over. Then klaxons honk, expletives sound, car doors slam, children wail, dogs yowl, ambulances whoop, police cars ululate, it's a Babel of frustration, a super-yawp of enforced procrastination.

They try to lift him, it's no good. There's nowhere to get a purchase. They try a scoop. No good either. The shovel blade can't get underneath him. They kick him. They wheedle. They implore. None of this has the slightest effect. Finally a resigned-looking constable gives the go-ahead simply to ignore him and the cars roll forward again, gingerly at first, and then more decisively, the drivers ignoring the slight jolt as the vehicles' tyres bump over Spider's body, flattening him inch by inch into the asphalt. Soon the road is smooth again, its polished camber abraded to a perfect curve. Spider is a star-shaped shadow in the centre of Eliot Boulevard, a complete nothing, as he would always have wanted.

Only at night, between the hours of three and four in the morning, is the street deserted. A mousing owl has strayed into the city and sits atop an ancient tree, looking down attentively at the shadow in the road. Something very curious is about to happen, but owls are not prone to astonishment. From time to time

they emit a low hoot, a signal of perfectly objective freedom. The kind of noise a car driver might make, were one to be liberated, suddenly, from roads.

Spider is peeling himself off the tarmac, with a sticky noise as of Elastoplast being removed from a wound. Slow or fast? That is the question. Spider does it slowly, as if to show appreciation, connoisseurship, of the predicament of adhesion. He has become elongated, an étoile wafer of unutterably slender spikiness. He resembles the punched-out noodle pastry shape of a spoke-radiant being from another planet. He glows slightly in the dark. Raised to the vertical, and poised for departure, he appears to await a signal.

The owl hoots.

Spider bumps away in the direction of anywhere that isn't Japan, a child's hoop, an old-fashioned cartwheel, not quite perfectly round, wobbling and swerving and lolloping from spoke to spoke, missing, of course, the felloe that would smoothe his circuitous departure.